SCREAMWORLD

When the insurance official sent to check out an accident at a gruesome theme park called Screamworld goes missing, private investigator John Brent is called in. Could the disappearance be linked with the unusual creator of the park — or are there other forces at work? What Brent finds behind the park's ghastly façade far exceeds his worst expectations, and threatens to drag him into a terrifying maelstrom of murder and madness, as the true purpose of the main attraction becomes all too clear . . .

Books by Edmund Glasby
in the Linford Mystery Library:

THE DYRYSGOL HORROR
THE ASH MURDERS
THE CHAOS OF CHUNG-FU
THE WEIRD SHADOW OVER
MORECAMBE
A MURDER MOST MACABRE
THE POSTBOX MURDERS
THE DOPPELGÄNGER DEATHS
ANGELS OF DEATH
WHERE BLOOD RUNS DEEP

EDMUND GLASBY

SCREAMWORLD

Complete and Unabridged

LINFORD
Leicester

First published in Great Britain

First Linford Edition
published 2018

A catalogue record for this book is available
from the British Library.

ISBN 978–1–4448–3666–0

1

A Bad Risk?

'Sorry to keep you waiting, John,' George Cavanagh apologised, setting the telephone receiver back into its cradle. He was the owner and managing director of Cavanagh Insurance, a large, exclusive and highly respected London-based firm of insurers who provided cover for a multitude of businesses. The greying hair he had left clung to his head like a tidemark, and his pale pudgy face was accentuated by the round glasses he wore. His expensive pin-striped suit was always immaculate, as were his highly polished shoes.

John Brent returned from examining one of the impressive paintings hung in the wood-panelled office and stood, perfectly at ease. There was a seat available for him at the desk, but he preferred to stand. 'That's quite all right, Mr Cavanagh. What can I do for you?'

'I'd like to hire you for a few days in order to investigate a disappearance.' Cavanagh pulled a slim folder towards himself but instead of opening it, he hesitated. 'I must tell you that this is rather different from the work you've done for us in the past. You've been of great help in exposing fraudulent claimants, and I've been impressed by how well you work with our own investigators.'

'They're good men,' Brent said politely. If truth be told, some of them were still wet behind the ears, and he had needed to give them a crash course in scepticism. A private investigator for over two decades, he had more experience than most, and over that time he had established a name for himself as having a sixth sense for liars.

'At the moment, there's one less of them.' Cavanagh sighed heavily.

Brent was surprised. 'It's one of your own investigators that's vanished?'

'Yes, two weeks ago, and I freely admit that I'm very worried about him.' Cavanagh opened the folder and drew out the top sheet of paper. 'These are the details of a policy that we took on six months ago. It provides full cover, all the usual details, to a funfair, or I think they call it an amusement park these days, in Gloucestershire.' He slid the paper to Brent. 'It's a fairly large set-up run by a Sicilian named Marco Scarvetti.'

'Scarvetti.' Brent thought for a moment. 'Isn't he the guy who used to direct low-budget horror films?'

'That's the one. He turned out over a dozen gore-laden pieces of cinematic trash; nasty pieces of work intended for the foreign markets. Fortunately, I've never seen any of them, and I doubt whether many people in this country have; for most, if not all of them, haven't got past the censors. Anyway, a couple of years ago he moved to Britain and decided to start up a fairground. A horror-themed fairground. It's known as Screamworld.'

'A sort of Boris Karloff-run Disneyland?' Brent quipped, smiling.

'Hardly. Like his films, it's pretty extreme. Some of the attractions are truly dreadful. Still, they draw the crowds.'

'I didn't know you insured anything like this,' said Brent, casting a cursory eye over the policy document.

'Against my better judgement, I'm afraid. The board have been wanting us to branch out for a while, and there have been a few new ventures on our part that I'm not entirely happy with. However, we did our site visits and got some data from within the industry to calculate the risks, and it all seemed to check out, so we set up the account and collected the premiums in due course. Then, about three weeks ago, I received a call from Scarvetti to say that there'd been an accident and they might need to pay compensation.'

'What happened?'

'A young woman broke both of her legs and severed her hand when the restraining bar on one of the whirligigs came loose. Naturally, we wanted to send someone down to check our liability, as we don't provide cover if the people running the rides are negligent. So McAlister paid them a visit.'

'James McAlister! He's the one who's missing?' Brent asked.

'Our best investigator, I'm sure you'd agree.'

Brent nodded. McAlister was professional: intelligent, thorough; and as suspicious a person as he was, they had got on well.

'McAlister interviewed the staff on the attraction as soon as he arrived and checked over their safety procedures. They were adamant that they'd done everything right.'

'What did Scarvetti have to say?'

'Not much. I've only spoken to him the once, but I didn't take to him.' Cavanagh took off his glasses and rubbed the bridge of his nose wearily.

'I take it McAlister suspected that Scarvetti was running the business badly, skimping on the safety measures? What was he going to do about it?'

'Check the entire funfair. If he could find examples of bad practice, we probably could've got out of paying and Scarvetti would've been landed with the costs. Then we'd also cancel his insurance. I approved the extra days the investigation would take and was looking forward to washing my hands of the whole affair. That, however, is when things turned murky. And, as you know, John, I don't like murkiness. Now, the police have verified that McAlister spent the following week going over the place with a fine-toothed comb. I didn't hear any more from him, as we'd arranged to meet here on the Monday. However, he never turned up.'

'And this was two weeks ago?' Brent asked. 'When were the police called in?'

'When McAlister missed our meeting, I asked my secretary to call his home number. His wife, Marie, didn't know where he was either. We all assumed that he'd been held up on the roads but when he still hadn't come home that night she called the police. They found his car a couple of days later, in Oxford of all places, and I'm afraid that they seem to have decided that he's not a real missing person. Apparently, someone there claims he was in the habit of visiting a woman, and they saw the two of them leave in her car.' Cavanagh shook his head firmly. 'Now, I know these things can happen, but McAlister isn't like that. He's a decent family man, devoted to his wife. I don't know if this is a genuine case of mistaken identity, or if the whole idea of a secret life has been cooked up on purpose, but as sure as I'm sitting here I know that something's wrong.'

'I assume the police made extensive enquiries at the funfair?'

'Cursory ones only. Scarvetti said that McAlister left on Friday as he'd told him he would. There was no sign of his belongings left in the bed and breakfast he'd been staying at, and the landlady confirms that he checked out on Friday morning.' Getting to his feet, Cavanagh pushed the folder across to Brent. 'I want you to find out what's going on. If there's enough evidence of wrongdoing, we might be able to get the police to sit up and take notice.'

Brent picked up the folder. 'You're worried Scarvetti's bumped him off, aren't you?' he asked bluntly.

'God help me, I am! And it was me who sent him there in the first place.'

'Any other leads?'

'Well, you might want to pay this man a visit.' Cavanagh scribbled down a name and a telephone number on a piece of paper and handed it over.

'Lionel Mellors?' Brent asked, reading

the note. 'Who's he?'

'Apparently he's an expert on Italian horror films and Scarvetti in particular. McAlister had intended to call in on him, but I don't think he ever got round to it. He's got a flat in Soho.'

'Okay. I'll try and arrange a meeting. Hopefully he'll see me today.'

'Be careful, John,' Cavanagh cautioned. 'I wouldn't trust Scarvetti as far as I could throw him. I don't want your disappearance on my conscience as well.'

Brent nodded his assent and said goodbye. Leaving the building, he felt a familiar surge of excitement and purpose, but for once it was tinged with something darker, something almost ominous.

* * *

The office in Heaton Gardens suited Brent admirably. It was in a quiet mews, but close enough to the centre that he could reach most parts of London quickly. The brass plate by the front entrance just had 'J.B. Investigations' written on it. Brent got most of his work through word of mouth and had never had to advertise.

He unlocked the door and stepped inside, switching on the lights. Four rooms led off the hall and each of the doors was wide open, as he had left them. He turned into the nearest room, where he kept a desk and several filing cabinets. The clean lines of his furniture were slightly marred by the many books filling the floor-to-ceiling shelves; an eclectic mix of reference books, fiction, biographies and technical manuals. A telephone and typewriter occupied part of the desk, but pride of place was given to a hefty marble pen and ink stand, with holders for both fountain pen and ballpoint. In truth, all of his correspondence and invoices were typed with carbon copies for his own reference, but he liked this nod to the past.

Setting down his briefcase on the desk, Brent opened it and removed the file that Cavanagh had given him. Despite the fact that it was mid-August, it was a dull day, so he switched on his desk lamp and started to read.

The first document was a standard policy insuring Scarvetti's Screamworld. It outlined the liabilities and detailed the exemptions. Nothing untoward there. Another slim section of papers comprised copies of the correspondence between Cavanagh Insurance and Scarvetti. He read these with interest, noting the slightly odd phrasing of Scarvetti's letters. If the man was born and raised in Italy, that would explain the idiosyncratic English. It gave the age and the name of the injured girl — nineteen-year-old Gillian West — and the name of the ride that had malfunctioned: The Horror. Then he reached the final section. This was a handwritten account from George Cavanagh himself, running to several pages. It set out all that he could remember of his conversations with McAlister, the information that the police had given to him and Marie McAlister, and his own unflattering opinion of Scarvetti.

The police involvement had indeed been cursory. McAlister's car had been found very quickly — too quickly? Brent wondered. Reading on, he saw why. The same person, Karen Garstang, who had said that McAlister was having an affair in Oxford, had reported the car for parking in her own space outside 78 Cromwell Street. A bit of a coincidence, that. He took a packet of cigarettes from his desk drawer and lit one. Garstang had told the police that McAlister had visited the area on several occasions to see a young woman called Helen Peterson who, it transpired, had subsequently cancelled her tenancy and left to travel round Europe. According to Garstang, McAlister had gone with her. The police had dropped the hunt shortly after that, having only visited the amusement park once to talk with Scarvetti. Apparently several people claimed that they saw McAlister leave the park on Friday morning, and a petrol attendant at a local garage confirmed that he had served the insurance investigator. There was nothing other than Cavanagh's instincts to tie Scarvetti to the disappearance.

Brent reached for the telephone and dialled Lionel Mellors's number.

★ ★ ★

Although he had lived in the capital for over thirty years, there were many parts of London Brent was unfamiliar with, Lionel Mellors's address in the middle of Soho, 4A Thornlow Street, being one of them. Once he had found somewhere convenient to park his silver Jaguar XJC Coupé, he consulted his street map, consigning the route to memory, coming to the conclusion that, given the confusing warren-like layout of one-way streets, it would make more sense to continue on foot. After he had locked the car, he paused for a moment to take in his squalid surroundings: the cheap bars, the strip show venues, the tattoo parlours and the dingy backstreet cinemas presenting X-rated films. The people on the streets reflected the sleazy urban environment: downtrodden, cheap and dodgy-looking. An unpleasant smell hung thickly in the air.

Despite the unsavoury locale, Brent was streetwise enough to know that, providing he just minded his own business, he was in no real danger. Crossing the street, he turned and entered a busy square, part of which was sectioned off. He could see a fat labourer, cigarette in mouth, shovel in hand, feeding a cement mixer. Noisy road maintenance works were taking place; workmen powering up pneumatic drills, breaking up the tarmac, all adding to the chaos. Leaving the bustling square, he soon found himself in a narrow, dingy backstreet, little more than an alley, in which scantily clad heavily made-up women and hard-faced men in cheap black suits — would-be gangsters — stood in darkened doorways. Paying them no heed, he continued until he came to a crossroads, where he then took a left turn and found himself at the edge of a tiny yet relatively well-tended park. Police sirens — the ever present sound of the city — warbled in the distance.

Mellors lived just up ahead. Skirting round the park, Brent headed for the house in question, surprised to see just how rundown it was. Given the area, he had not expected to find a grand abode set within acres of grounds; yet it did not seem fitting for someone who was renowned as a leading authority on Italian cinema. Unless the film buff chose to live here for reasons known only to himself, there was clearly little money to be made in that particular field of study.

4A Thornlow Street was a basement flat. Brent went down the uneven steps, noting the blackness beyond the sole dirty window. An old bike with a punctured front tyre leant against the wall next to a rubbish bin. He knocked loudly on the blue-painted door. For a while there was no answer. Mellors had sounded reasonably 'with it' on the phone, and Brent hoped that the other had remembered this afternoon's meeting and had not gone out.

A toilet flushed somewhere inside, followed moments later by an outburst of coughing. Then came the ponderous shuffling of approaching feet. A bolt was drawn back and the door opened. Lionel Mellors stood in the doorway. He was a tall, grey-haired, dishevelled man; his clothes crumpled and unwashed. A small pair of half-moon spectacles hung on a thin chain around his long, deeply wrinkled neck. He looked tired and unwell. 'Yes?'

'Mr Mellors? I'm John Brent.'

'Oh yes, please, come in.' Mellors took a couple of steps back, allowing his guest to enter.

'It's very kind of you to see me at such short notice,' Brent said. He closed the door and found himself in a dimly lit hall.

'This way.'

Following Mellors, Brent entered a large study. There was a desk and two chairs but little else in the way of actual furniture. Shelves crammed with files, reference books and numerous fading posters of old films dominated the walls. Much of the uncarpeted floor space was similarly taken up with piled boxes, all labelled. A mustiness hung in the air, catching at the back of his throat.

'Please, take a seat.'

Eyes roving around the myriad contents of the room, Brent sat down in the chair Mellors gestured to.

'So you want to know about Marco Scarvetti?' Mellors sat down opposite and interlaced his long nicotine-stained fingers.

'Yes. I understand you're an expert on him.'

'Well I don't know if I'd go that far, but I do indeed know much about him.' Mellors coughed and leaned back in his chair. 'Several years ago I began work on a detailed biography of the man, but alas I never got round to completing it. I did compile a list of every known film he was involved with and did a lot of the preliminary research into his life. However, one thing led to another, and the project was never finished.'

'Did he make many films?'

'About three hundred.'

'Three *hundred*?'

'Yes, but some of them are only a few minutes long. Nowadays, people only associate him with the splatterfest horrors for which he's become infamous. The so-called *gialli* and *mondo* films; low-budget shockers such as *Death Will Eat You*, *Zombie Lovers* and *The Graveyard Feasters*.'

'Unusual titles! Have you ever met him?'

16

'No, not personally. It's a lifelong ambition that I'd one day get to meet him; and now that he's moved to Britain, who knows? However, due to my ailing health I don't get out much.' Mellors coughed violently into his hand, his shoulders lurching, spittle leaking from between his fingers.

Brent waited until the other had regained some composure. 'What can you tell me about him as a person — his past in particular?'

'While it's hard to find biographical information relating to Marco Scarvetti, this is what I've been able to piece together over the years. He was born in Palermo, Sicily in 1906 to Edgardo and Isabella Scarvetti. His father was a peasant fisherman who was conscripted to fight the Austrian-Hungarians during the First World War and who died in 1915 at the battle of Isonzo River. His mother passed away two years later from a rare parasitic infection attributed to bad shellfish. He also had an uncle living in Messina who had strong Mafia ties. Anyway, young Marco was taken in by an order of monks at the nearby hilltop monastery of Santa Benedicti. He stayed there — ' Mellors broke into a further bout of coughing. 'Excuse me,' he said, taking a sip of water from a glass.

'He stayed there for a further seven years. What exactly happened there is a mystery. However, I think it fair to say that his monastic experience was far from a happy one. There are several portrayals of the clergy in his films, none of them complimentary. In fact, far from it. They're all depicted as hypocritical child abusers who usually end up dying in the most violent manner. A prime example being the fate of the priests in *The Stigmata of Satan*, which, believe me, has to be seen to be believed. How he got away with it, I don't know. Anyway, by 1924 and now a young adult, Scarvetti fled the monastery, rejecting the faith that others had tried to beat into him. Homeless and destitute, he — ' His account was punctuated again by an outburst of coughing.

'He wandered the streets of his home town before stowing away on a ship bound for Tangiers in 1926. What happened to him whilst in North Africa is unknown, however there must have been a complete reversal in fortune, for by the time he returned to Italy in the early 1930s he was no longer penniless. In fact, he was sitting on a considerable private fortune.'

Brent looked up from the notebook he had been scribbling some of the details in. 'No idea as to how he made his money?'

'None. Maybe he found a gold mine or started up a slave trade. Maybe his uncle helped him out; set him up in some kind of illicit business. Pimping or gun running. From the rumours I've heard, it seems likely, but who knows?'

'A bit nefarious, our Mr Scarvetti, is he?'

'This is but pure speculation. And besides, it was over forty years ago. However, there's no denying that what came next did border on the criminal, but I'll get to that later.' Mellors took another sip of water and put the glass down.

'Throughout the 1930s, he ran various businesses all loosely connected with the Italian film industry. He experimented with different types of cinematography, mastering the use of the hand-held Kinamo camera before going on to work extensively with the Super 8 format. Fleeing Mussolini's grip on the island, Scarvetti used his contacts and his money to secure passage to America, establishing himself as a film director in New York in 1941. He stayed there for ten years, perfecting his talents and rubbing shoulders with many young upcoming directors, before returning to Italy with an American wife — Elizabeth Hastings — and a three-year-old son, called Viscero, in tow. Throughout the mid- to late 1950s, his output was tremendous, and it was about this time that he established a name for himself as a film director who was prepared to go to extremes.'

'How extreme?' Brent asked.

'Basically, there were no limits to what he would or wouldn't do. I believe he saw it as his almost sacred duty to instil as much fear and horror in his audience as he could. To give you some idea of the man's, dare I say, genius . . . In 1960 he organised an expedition to South America; the Brazilian rainforest I believe. There he shot a documentary — or rather, a shockumentary — of a hitherto undiscovered cannibal tribe. Three members of his crew, including his wife, were killed in the making of the film; devoured by the tribe. Their grisly deaths Scarvetti captured on celluloid and released.'

'And there was me thinking it couldn't get any worse,' Brent commented dryly.

'The footage was supposedly destroyed. However, rumour persists that a copy's still out there somewhere, perhaps mouldering in someone's attic. It's what those in the industry refer to as a 'snuff' film. Scarvetti narrowly avoided criminal charges, no doubt thanks to 'Family' connections. A string of horror greats such as *Red Splotches, Cannibal Islanders, Flesh!* and *Daddy, Why Won't It Die?* came out in the mid-1960s. Then, completely out of the blue, Scarvetti flipped.'

'You mean . . . he went mad?'

'Exactly that. He was committed to an insane asylum, spent a couple of years inside and then was let out, supposedly cured. His last film, *The Lazarus Cult*, was never released. For reasons unknown, he abandoned his studios in Rome and came to England in order to open a funfair. How bizarre is that?'

★　★　★

The journey west was uneventful, and Brent reached the outskirts of Oxford shortly after five o'clock that afternoon. He pulled up outside a newsagent's in Headington and bought a map of the city, finding the address, 78 Cromwell Street, with the help of the shopkeeper who directed him to a street lined with terraced houses. After he had found somewhere to park up, he approached the house and knocked on the door.

There was no answer. Peering through the window, Brent could see no signs of occupancy. The place looked deserted.

A voice called from across the street. Surprised, Brent turned to see a stooped elderly man with white hair, spectacles and a walking stick.

'If you're looking for Miss Garstang, I'm afraid you're too late. She's left.'

'You mean she's out?'

'No. She's moved. Left the country, I believe.' The stranger hobbled forward.

'I don't suppose you'd know if she's left a forwarding address?'

'Not as far as I'm aware. She hadn't lived here long.'

'Oh?'

'Yes, a funny woman that; friendly one day, ignored you the next. I always try to welcome our new residents, get them to feel part of the community, but she didn't want to know. Of course, I might have frightened her off. Not everyone wants to be bothered with their neighbours.'

'When did she leave?' Brent asked.

'Cleared out two days ago. Lock, stock and barrel. The police came to see her before that. Apparently they'd found a missing car outside her house.'

'Actually, that's what I was going to ask her about.'

'Why, are you a copper?'

'No . . . I'm a friend of the car's owner. He's vanished.'

'Oh dear! I hadn't realised it was anything serious.'

'The police took a statement from Miss Garstang where she claimed the car had been left here on several occasions and that my friend was having an affair with the young woman at number sixty.'

'Well, that's certainly not true! I noticed the car myself, as it was parked really badly, right up on the pavement, but I'd never seen it before then. It probably sounds like I'm the worst kind of nosy parker, but I do like to keep an eye on the street. If I'd known who owned that car, I'd have had a word; and as to the other . . . matter. Helen Peterson, who lives at number sixty, is a confirmed spinster who regularly goes off travelling. I'm afraid that Miss Garstang must have got it very wrong.'

'What's she like, this Karen Garstang?'

'Flashy. Good-looking in a tarty sort of way; imagine a dark-haired Bet Lynch from *Coronation Street*. Lots of make-up and jewellery. I'll tell you another thing: whatever she said about being from the Midlands, she wasn't British. Spanish or Italian would be my guess, though why she'd want to keep it quiet I don't know. Funny woman.'

2

All the Fun of the Fair

It was approaching nine o'clock in the evening, and the skies were darkening, when Brent finally found Screamworld. Despite the fact that it was well sign-posted, it was stuck out in the middle of nowhere; and whilst there were one or two villages within walking distance, it was far enough away from any larger centres of population to make him wonder how exactly it attracted custom. There was an expansive carpark, half-empty; but given the fact that it was a weekday and that the forecast was for heavy showers, that was of no real surprise. Crossing the carpark, he saw an especially laid-on bus arrive. The vehicle pulled up, and a disorderly mob of foul-mouthed teenagers poured out before making a mad dash for the entrance.

Brent paused for a moment, waiting for

them to buy their tickets, taking in the frightening imagery that adorned the opening to the fairground. With some level of amazement, he gazed at the monstrous horned sculpture that reared high above him: part man, part beast, what looked like layers of stretched skin and gore spanned its partially skeletal framework, and from its body protruded a leg and cloven hoof which, due to its raised angle, gave the thing the semblance of dynamism, as though it were about to haul itself free from its containment and rampage across the land. Its eye sockets were empty and cavernous; dark holes set within the red-stained skull. The entrance itself was via that skull. The fearsome fang-filled jaws, although open wide, gave the uncomfortable impression that at any moment they would clamp down on the unwary.

Arching over the sculpture, a huge sign in large red brushstrokes read: SCREAM-WORLD. Brent stepped inside.

Thanks to a considerable amount of cosmetics, the man in the ticket booth looked like something that had just crawled from a crypt; scabrous and bloody. His face was painted a ghastly green, and a pair of ill-fitting false teeth enhanced his ghoulish appearance. With no intention of actually going on any of the attractions, Brent paid for admission only. Then, once he had his pass, he stepped inside, the relatively sane world outside transforming almost instantaneously into one of exuberant, macabre madness. It must have been close on forty years since he had last visited a funfair, certainly before the outbreak of the Second World War, and things had certainly come on leaps and bounds in that time. There was no denying the fact that a lot of money had been invested in the amusement park; a far cry from the travelling fairs that used to set up in a field near his home town.

Conspicuously absent were the familiar Ferris wheel and the carousel, these rides clearly eclipsed by the newer crowd-pulling attractions — highlighting the fact that the more genteel things that may have entertained previous generations held no interest whatsoever for the modern thrill-seekers.

Taking in his surroundings with an

observant eye, Brent saw straight ahead a veritable eyesore called The Meat Grinder: a huge black and red vaguely octopoid machine that whirled its passengers around at a furious pace, inverting and spinning them like some futuristic monster. To his right was a large dodgem ride arena named The Vampire's Vortex; the speeding vehicles, designed to resemble huge bats, colliding with bone-jarring intensity. To his immediate left was a range of fast food stalls. His rumbling stomach reminded him that he had not eaten since lunch, and he walked over and ordered himself a hamburger.

Made up to look like one of the living dead, the bored obese woman behind the counter took his money, reached into a heated glass cabinet and removed a ready-made hamburger, which she passed over. Brent looked dubiously at his snack, his nose wrinkling with disgust upon seeing the bright yellow mustard and watery tomato sauce that oozed from inside, staining the paper napkin. He had eaten some garbage in his time as a private investigator, particularly when stuck in a greasy spoon café waiting for a suspect to leave a building nearby. He knew the horror of finding a used plaster in the last mouthful of his meal. But this poor excuse for a hamburger was pushing the edges of his personal line in the sand. There was a soggy feel to it; and as he took it in his grip, his fingers sank obscenely into the sesame seed bun, ejecting a sickly gout of grease that squelched and landed in a small puddle at his feet, narrowly missing his shoes. Tentatively raising the top layer of the bun, he saw that the meat was bloody, certainly undercooked, if not raw. With a curse, he glared at the vendor, thought about starting an argument, then turned his back and tossed the takeaway into a waste bin. A few wasps rose briefly from the leftover candyfloss, and he was struck by the sickly-sweet smell of the spun sugar.

There were three tiers of smell that he could detect. The most obvious was that of food: the fried onions, the hot dogs, the toffee apples and other jaw-stickers that the fairground sold in abundance. Underneath that was the smell of people — sweat, tears and the nauseating lingering scent of vomit from those who could not stomach the more violent rides. Underlying it all, however, was the smell of diesel and oil; grimy machinery constantly turning and creating its own miasma of inhuman industry.

Brent stepped away from the bin and ventured further into the fairground, judgementally assessing the crowded, smelly, noisy, oppressive horror-themed chaos. The noise grew: almost deafening music blaring from the savage round-abouts and the death-defying swings; great waves of sound clashing discordantly, beating against the ears. There was a sudden whoosh directly behind him and the rattle of wheels on rails. Turning his head, he saw a hearse-like carriage race past thirty feet above him, its four occupants screaming with a mix of excitement and fear as they rode a rickety wooden rollercoaster called The Death Trap. There was a horrible-looking hall of mirrors, a revolving cage, a waltzer, a gruesome ghost-train-like attraction, and a vertigo-inducing hundred-and-twenty-foot-high tower named Satan's Downfall up which a large seating platform was elevated and then, once it had reached the top, allowed to drop, simulating a freefall experience. Everything about Screamworld looked stomach-churning.

Nonchalantly, Brent walked over to a range of nearby stalls, unsurprised to see that even the classic hook-a-duck, the tin-can alley, the coconut shy and the shooting gallery had been horribly transformed. For here was a range at which bloodthirsty youngsters were behaving like Amazonian natives, shooting darts from blowpipes at a rack of plastic shrunken heads, crying out with joy whenever their missiles struck home. The prizes on offer were equally macabre — creepy-looking fetish-like dolls, dark Tarot decks, wax skulls, hideous masks and the like.

'Five pence for three throws,' touted one of the barkers, offering to any takers a dripping red sponge as though it were a bloody heart freshly plucked from a sacrificed victim. 'A prize every time.'

At the stall in question, Brent could see a moving screen plastered in splotches of sticky crimson. Monstrous beings had been painted thereon; face holes revealing flesh and blood fairground workers — the targets for the saturated projectiles. Anywhere else, such a form of 'entertainment' could have been considered light-hearted and indeed frivolous, but here things were different. This was no clowns throwing bags of water at each other or 'soak the teacher'. To Brent's mind, it was too grisly for starters. And whilst the hurled sponges obviously inflicted no physical harm, they implied a greater level of violence, leaving shotgun-blast-like marks wherever they hit. With a wry grin, he noticed that the attraction was called Blood and Guts. One lucky teenager had won big and pushed his way through the crowd, grinning triumphantly as he hefted a black infant-sized coffin crammed with goodies over his shoulder.

Shaking his head with disbelief, Brent walked on. He could not decide whether Scarvetti was a true genius in the sense that he had established a genuine money-spinning enterprise, or whether he belonged back in the mental institute. It was a close call, for it was indisputable that Scream-world was the product of a disturbed mind; indeed a sick mind. Yet, was it not the case in some instances that madness and inventiveness went hand in hand? It was a documented fact that many of the world's greatest artists were a few sandwiches short of a picnic.

The rearing shape of another huge revolving monstrous contraption lay directly ahead. Weird lighting gave its metallic arms and body an unsettling, almost dripping look as it spun slowly and ponderously, before accelerating to a breakneck speed against the growing darkness. The noise that accompanied it was tremendous. Brent saw the sign: The Zombie Maker. Judging by the dizzy white-faced state of those coming off the ride, he thought it aptly named.

'Hey, mister.'

Brent turned at the tap on his shoulder. The man before him was perhaps several years older than himself and dressed in a long weather-beaten raincoat. Hirsute, unkempt, unwashed and underfed, he could quite easily be one of the vagrants he had seen in some of the slummier parts of London. There was a mad look in his red-rimmed eyes, and he stank of stale beer.

'If you don't want it, do you mind if I have it?' The stranger held out the discarded hamburger he had obviously scavenged from the waste bin. 'Normally I wouldn't ask, but you look the kind who might take offence.'

Brent's initial sense of shock turned to mild guilt. Unlike him, this unfortunate could not be choosy as to what he ate. 'Sure, be my guest.'

'Thanks.' With a hungry bite, the man took a messy mouthful. With three such bites, he had devoured the hamburger and began wiping his greasy fingers on his coat. He spat and cursed vehemently as a large gang of adolescents rushed past, shouting and swearing.

'I take it you don't like kids either,' said Brent conversationally.

'Used to. Don't anymore.'

Brent smiled. 'I guess we were all young once.'

'Young, yes, I'll give you that; but we had more respect back then.' The man glared at the teenagers. 'I had to throw kids off my ride every weekend for messing about, and they'd swear like you'd never believe.'

'You work here?' Brent was surprised.

'Not for a while. Had to give it up for my health. Though I still come and see the old place sometimes,' the vagrant continued. 'Talk to my mates, you know. There's good pickings here, like your burger. Big Sue makes a great burger. You don't know what you're missing!' He grinned and shambled off.

'A trip to hospital most likely,' Brent muttered under his breath. He found himself wondering how the presence of someone like this was tolerated in the fairground. Did the owner feel sorry for this wreck of a man and let him wander around, scavenging from the discarded leftovers? He watched him head to another rubbish bin where things were quieter and begin scrabbling through it. He was a pathetic figure, but the fact that he was an ex-employee might prove useful. He was going to have to be careful in his enquiries, and the chance to talk to anyone who used to work for Scarvetti was not one he should pass up.

He watched the man fish out a

crumpled cigarette packet and then throw it to one side with a curse. Past experience had taught him the value of what he termed the 'gutter gossip' — the lead from the streets; and while he was not always at ease dealing with such people, it was undeniable that their knowledge could prove invaluable, providing they could be persuaded to talk. Drink often did the trick, but in this potential informant's case maybe a different kind of temptation would work better. Besides, there was a strict no-alcohol ban in place in the theme park.

'Want a smoke?' he asked, walking over and holding one of his own cigarettes out.

The man spun round and smiled, revealing several gaps in his discoloured teeth. 'Don't mind if I do.' Taking the cigarette, he lit up with obvious pleasure. 'What are you doing here, anyway? You don't seem the usual type.'

'I don't?' Brent answered, lighting his own cigarette. Given the nature of his surroundings and the present company, he took it as a compliment.

'Nah.' The man shook his head. 'Too old to go on the rides yourself. No bit of stuff to impress by winning a prize. No kiddies, not that this place gets many of them anyway. Anyhow, the name's Fred. Fred Haddow.'

'Well, Fred, what is it with this horror theme? A bit over the top, wouldn't you say?' Brent took a drag on his cigarette.

'That's Spaghetti's idea; the boss man.'

'Spaghetti? What kind of name's that?' Brent exclaimed.

'Well, it's something like that. I never could get his name right. He's well into the horror stuff, though. Well into it. He said that it'd pull in the teenagers. Said they'd fall for anything like that. The bloodier the better.' Haddow puffed on his cigarette. 'I think he wants every night to be like Halloween. Heard tell he even tried to get Christopher Lee to come to the big opening, told him he'd fly him in special on his private helicopter, but he didn't fancy it.'

A vision of the actor in his full Count Dracula costume cutting a ribbon came to Brent's mind. 'Well, it would've made a memorable event,' he commented. He had been dragged along by a friend to see the Hammer Film production *Dracula A.D. 1972* when it had been released a few years previously and had found it mildly entertaining, if somewhat preposterous.

'I don't like that stuff much personally, trying to scare people. But a job's a job, right?'

'Did you like working here?' Brent asked casually, pleased that the conversation was going in a helpful direction.

Haddow shrugged, his scrawny shoulders rising to his ears. 'Suppose so. Long hours and annoying kids, but it could've been worse. It was better than not having a job.' He looked restless and was peering around. 'I'd best be off out of here. Don't want to outstay my welcome, if you know what I mean. Thanks for the smoke . . . and the burger.'

'Before you go, do you mind telling me where I can find The Horror?'

Haddow pointed. 'See where the funhouse is — the one with Spaghetti's mug on it? Take a right and you can't miss it.' His directions given, he cast a furtive look around and skulked away.

Brent took a further drag on his cigarette, then threw it to the ground. Heading for the grotesquely decorated building his ragged informant had identified as the funhouse, he became increasingly aware of the sly stares thrown his way by some of the stallholders and attraction operators. Contemplating the dark possibility that, having been seen with Haddow, he was now under surveillance, he kept his eyes open for any signs of potential threat. A light, steady drizzle began to fall.

'Jesus Christ,' Brent muttered to himself as he gazed with some measure of revulsion at the three-storey funhouse. He was now able to discern its true name, for it was written in large messy brushstrokes above the entrance — Welcome to my Madness. The building's exterior was covered with a glowing, glistening blood-and-green-slime-soaked montage of terrible images taken largely from Scarvetti's own films: flesh-eating monsters, demons from the blackest pits, and amorphous Lovecraftian horrors. Crowning the building was a large billboard upon which was painted a larger-than-life-sized portrait; the face that of a dark-haired, thin-faced, hollow-eyed man, slightly demonic in appearance. There was little doubt that it was Scarvetti.

Brent could see that there was a small booth at the entrance. Someone dressed as Death — black cloak, skeleton costume, authentic-looking scythe and skull mask — sat inside. 'Death' saw the private investigator and beckoned him over with a skeletal finger.

Slightly unnerved, Brent waved his hand, signalling the fact that he had no interest in entering. Even if the heavens were to open and the rain to start falling in torrents, he doubted whether he would be fool enough to go inside. How on earth anyone could willingly go in there was beyond him. No doubt it was just filled with wobbling staircases, slides, shifting walkways, secret doors, revolving drums and dark passages lit with sporadic strobe lighting; but nevertheless there was something about it that made him uneasy. He found his eyes being drawn almost hypnotically to the large painting of the fairground owner, noting the cold, sardonic smile on his lips and the gleam in his dark, piercing eyes. Strangely, he found himself taking a step forward. Then another.

Having now been debouched from one ride, a rowdy gang of youngsters ran by, heading for something else. Brent jolted out of his daze, surprised to find that he was now only a few steps away from 'Death'. Rubbing his temple confusedly, he shook his head and backtracked. Unsure as to what had temporarily come over him, he made his way towards The Horror — an indoor dark ride that took its passengers through an infernal labyrinth of twists and turns, sudden drops, scares and frights. It was on this that Gillian West had sustained her life-changing injuries. From what he had read about the attraction in Cavanagh's notes, parts of it were also peopled with human actors dressed up as ghosts, vampires and rubber axe- and chainsaw-wielding psychopaths that sprang out on the unwary at unsuspecting moments, upping the fear factor. It was undoubtedly not for the faint-hearted, and it would have been invaluable to find out what McAlister had thought of it. There was a large queue of people waiting to go on.

Trying to look inconspicuous, although he was only too aware that both his age and his formal attire made him stand out like a sore thumb, Brent walked over. From a distance, he gazed at the single-seater cars, noting the restraining bars that kept their passengers secure — or were at least supposed to. He assumed that after the young woman's accident, they had been stringently tested to ensure no future mishaps occurred. The zombie-masked operator looked competent enough, and he was giving each bar a manual check before sending the cars on their way.

Brent lit another cigarette, pondering his next move. There was little doubt that this ride, and this fairground, had been the focus of McAlister's own investigation, though that in itself did not imply that his disappearance was in any way related specifically to it. He could have found out something else; for instance a piece of incriminating evidence about Scarvetti's past. Given what Mellors had revealed, that seemed fairly likely. His lips creased into a smile at the thought of the Sicilian's numerous skeletons crawling from their proverbial cupboards and being put on display inside his attractions.

As forecast, the rain was becoming heavier. Brent was now getting wet. Trying to keep a low profile, he passed the queue and went around the side of The Horror. It was basically rectangular in layout, thirty-five feet tall, covering an area perhaps a sixth that of a football pitch. Like many of the other rides, its outer design was heavily horror-themed. A metal fence barred any further exploration, preventing him from seeing what was at the back. Peering through the gaps in the railing, he saw nothing untoward.

'Are you looking for something?'

Brent spun on his heel. Two men in dark grey, full-length raincoats stood before him. One was tall and burly, bald-headed and unshaven, and from the looks of him quite capable of and willing to dish out a good deal of bodily harm to anyone he did not like. The other man was shorter, wore glasses and had a distinctly olive cast to his skin. Both reeked of menace.

'Yes . . . I was looking for the . . . toilets.'

'The toilets?' queried the man with the glasses.

'Yes. I thought I saw a sign pointing this way.' Brent noticed the slight bulge in the bigger man's coat, right about where a gun could be concealed.

The shorter man eyed him suspiciously. 'The toilets are back that way. Near the entrance. There's nothing around here.'

Brent took his cigarette from his mouth and blew out a column of smoke. 'Thanks.' With a nod of appreciation, he began walking away, trying to appear calm. After thirty or so unhurried steps, he looked back over his shoulder and was not surprised to see that the two men were fixedly watching his progress. Soon he was weaving his way through a throng of teenagers, and then he was passing The Zombie Maker.

A truly hideous cacophony of high-pitched screams rent the night, distinguishable from the other yells by their genuine terror-laden intensity. For whereas the other cries were those generated by a pleasurable, anticipated rush of adrenaline, these were ones of stark-raving fear; primal and dark.

There was something wrong here. Of that Brent was certain. Never had he heard anyone or anything utter such a ghastly sound. He stood, temporarily riveted to the spot, as a crowd of youngsters ran past, clamouring to get away from whatever spectacle was playing out some distance ahead.

That terrible scream was repeated, and then from out of the ensuing chaos there staggered a man, arms extended, face twitching spasmodically. His clothes were blackened as though covered in soot, but his hair and skin were, like his eyes, which had rolled back in his head, chalk-white. Yellow foam-flecked goo bubbled and leaked from his closed mouth. Shaking violently, the unfortunate crumpled to the ground.

Brent's initial thought was that the man was having some kind of fit. He rushed over and crouched down, reluctant to come into contact with the powdery black residue. What first aid he knew, basically how to treat cuts and burns, would be of little help here, and he was alarmed to see that the casualty had now ceased shaking and had gone limp. Checking for a pulse, he was relieved to feel a quickened throb. It was faster than what he had expected, but at least it signalled that the man was alive.

'We'll take it from here.'

Looking up, the private investigator saw the short man with the glasses. He had been joined by another man who, from his undead disguise, was probably the operator of one of the rides. 'He needs to get to hospital. Urgently.' Brent stood up. He could see more men arriving. Long-coated men.

'And he will, I assure you. Now, if you'll just stand aside.'

Reluctantly, Brent backed away. He watched, curious, as within moments the prone body was concealed by a ring of men, none of whom looked like an emergency first-aider. The short man then gave some orders and the body was lifted and carried off. Realising that he was unlikely to get any answers from these people, Brent went over to a group of teenagers who were watching the proceedings with shocked eyes. 'Did anyone see what happened?' he asked.

'He . . . he came off The Horror. And he . . . ' a girl in tears mumbled.

'I think he was electrocuted,' said a ginger-haired kid, picking his nose.

'Yeah, he looked all burnt-up,' agreed a lanky teenager with a safety pin through his nose and short spiky hair.

Wiping the rain from his eyes, Brent made his way back towards the attraction. The crowds had thinned out considerably, and even the deafening music seemed to have died down. Aside from a group of milling 'long-coats', The Horror ride was now devoid of thrill-seekers. The gathered men seemed worried and confused, their attention focused on one of the single-seater cars.

It looked like Cavanagh Insurance would soon be facing another claim from Scarvetti's Screamworld.

3

Strange Invitations

The somewhat grand hotel Brent had chosen was several miles from Scream-world. He went down to breakfast early and then seated himself in the lounge to gather his thoughts and write up his findings to date. As usual, he made a neat list of the important points and how far he had got in tackling them. The information from Oxford was interesting, but at the moment it could take him no further. His initial impressions of the amusement park and its staff were unfavourable, but he would need to find evidence to substantiate his instincts. To keep it fresh in his memory, he wrote down a description of the 'electrocuted' unfortunate.

How could it have happened? Had the man climbed out of his carriage and got in among the ride; perhaps brushed against a faulty power cable? Or had the accident occurred while he was still in his seat? Brent would have thought that after the Gillian West incident, measures would have been taken to prevent any further mishaps. He stared out of the window, vaguely registering the neatly gravelled driveway at the front of the hotel. His mind was filled with the sights and sounds of the previous night: the noisy funfair, the ghoulish images drawing people to the attractions, the look of horror on the man's face and the strange yellow froth that had leaked from his mouth.

Then there were the rather sinister 'long-coats'. What function did they serve? Park security, perhaps? He wrote quickly, eager to get his ideas down on paper, even if they proved to be groundless. Had this ever happened before? Which company had provided Scarvetti with insurance prior to Cavanagh's involvement? How could he find out where the victim was now and how he was? Did any of these things have a bearing on McAlister's disappearance?

Voices drifted in from the dining room, but Brent ignored them. He kept on working, going over the possibilities until it was late enough to call Cavanagh. Going up to his room, he hung the 'do not disturb' sign on the door handle and put a call through to London. The secretary confirmed that her boss had just arrived, and a moment later Cavanagh was on the line.

'Ah, John! What do you have for me?' Cavanagh asked eagerly.

'Well, I'm fairly certain that we can discount the theory that McAlister was having an affair — that's pure fabrication to my mind; a blind alley. That said, I'd still be interested to know what Karen Garstang has to do with this. She's apparently left the area under somewhat suspicious circumstances, and it would be difficult to track her down. I can try, but — '

'No. At least not at the moment,' Cavanagh interrupted. 'If you think that's a waste of time, I'll trust your judgement. What about Scarvetti's blasted theme park? Have you been there?'

'Yes, last night, and so far I concur with McAlister's opinion that it's poorly run.

It's clearly making a lot of money, but I'd say it could well be unsafe.' Brent related all he had seen, ending with the incident on The Horror.

Cavanagh groaned. 'Oh Christ! Not another claim! What on earth are they doing there?'

'That's what I plan to discover. The question is, how do you want me to go about it? I can achieve a certain amount covertly, but I can't actually interview Scarvetti and his staff without some kind of mandate. I could use a cover story if you like, reporter or something similar, or I can go straight in as a representative of Cavanagh Insurance, picking up from where McAlister left off. However, that might carry its own risks.'

There was a pause as Cavanagh considered his options. He cleared his throat. 'For now, I'd like you to stay anonymous. Perhaps ask around locally to see what people think of this Scarvetti's Screamworld; see if you can find out anything about the latest incident. Surely there'll be something about it in the local press?'

'Possibly, although it's rather early for that. It's only been a few hours,' Brent commented. 'I also have no name for the victim, in order to check the hospitals.'

'I may be able to give you that soon, if it doesn't come to light in the papers. Scarvetti was pretty quick to call me when the girl got injured. How should I contact you if I've any information?'

'Just leave a message on this number asking me to phone you. In fact, I was going to ask you something anyway. Do you know who was insuring Scarvetti before you?'

'I can't remember off the top of my head, but it should be in the files,' Cavanagh said. 'I take it you'd like to know if there have been any prior claims on the park's insurance?'

'That's right. It's been going for a few years now, and I'd be surprised if it's only just slipped into bad practices.' Brent looked through his notes. 'There was one other thing I was going to ask. Do you have a home address for Scarvetti?'

'Yes, hang on a moment. I made a note of it yesterday. It's an Italian-sounding place.' There was a rustling on the line as Cavanagh shuffled through some papers. 'Here it is. Casa Degli Orrori, Barrows Lane, Furneaux. I think it's pretty near the amusement park.'

'Thanks, that could be useful.' Brent noted down the address, checking the spelling back. 'Casa Degli Orrori. That's 'House of Horror', isn't it?'

'Wouldn't surprise me.'

'Well, I think that's all for now, Mr Cavanagh.'

'Right. Good hunting, John.' Cavanagh rang off.

Brent put the receiver down and stretched out on the bed, hands behind his head. He still had no clear plan of attack, but some possibilities were forming in his mind. Screamworld did not open until noon, even during the holidays, so that was out for the morning. A visit to Scarvetti's house was tempting, as was the idea of sounding out local people to get their views on the gruesome addition to their area.

Swinging his legs off the bed, he stood up, his mind decided. He would canvas opinion about Screamworld and its owner first. The hotel was some distance from the amusement park, but he had seen a leaflet advertising it in the reception area. He straightened his tie and smoothed down his dark hair, looking every bit the suave and sophisticated man that he was. The sprinkling of grey that had appeared a few years ago suited him and leant a little gravitas to his good looks. The receptionist had taken a shine to him when she had seen him at breakfast. It should be easy enough to start a conversation about the amusement park and find out if there were any rumours regarding it. He guessed that many people must have had strong objections to the place, with its garish and ghoulish imaginings of a horror film director. Not exactly an obvious attraction for middle England.

There was nothing like indignation to make people gossip.

* * *

'I know the council thought it would be a good idea, but that was when it was going to be a normal funfair. At least it's not that close to the city but really, it's such an eyesore. And the people who go there . . . well!' The receptionist, a grey-haired woman with bright blue eyes, was only too happy to talk about Screamworld. One casual question from Brent about whether he should take his young nephews there had opened the floodgates to a river of complaints. 'We get a lot of bikers through here now looking for it, and coach-loads of teenagers. God only knows where they all come from.'

'It must be good for business, though.'

'Not ours, it isn't. We cater for nice people; professionals and families. The types who visit Screamworld don't stay here. There's a caravan site and some cheap guesthouses closer to it. What we do get, sometimes, is half-drunk idiots who want to come into the bar late at night. The manager, Mr Warren, has had to call the police on several occasions in order to have them removed.'

Brent shook his head in disapproval. 'All the same, it must've provided some jobs for local people.'

'A few,' the receptionist admitted

grudgingly. 'Not as many as you might think, though. The owner brought a lot of his own men with him. Italians, I believe.'

'Oh yes, there was a bit in the leaflet about him.' Brent scanned the glossy flyer, pretending to search for the name. 'Here it is — 'World-famous horror auteur Marco Scarvetti brings together the most terrifying rides in Europe. Dare you face Screamworld?' Yes, I think it wouldn't be appropriate for the boys. At eight and eleven, they're too young for this kind of thing.'

'Definitely. I just hope we can get rid of it soon.' The woman shuffled the leaflets on her desk and began picking out some attractions suitable for families. 'Since a girl got hurt there a few weeks ago, some of the locals have started a campaign to get the place shut down.'

'Do you think they could be success-ful?' Brent asked.

The receptionist pursed her lips and considered. 'Maybe, but it would take a long time. Unless there's a real tragedy there, of course; and I pray to God that doesn't happen.' She pushed her glasses back onto the bridge of her nose, a habitual movement by the look of it. 'For the life of me, I can't think why that horrible man chose to come and build his abomination here! It really is a blight on the landscape. It does nothing but give this place a bad name.'

The conversation then moved on to other local attractions, and finally Brent was able to get away. Back in his room, he reflected on that very question. What had caused Scarvetti to leave Italy in the first place? Could he have been in trouble with the law? And why Britain? Why not somewhere in the United States, for example? As far as he was aware, Gloucestershire had no prior connection with horror movies. He felt frustrated. He was becoming increasingly certain that McAlister's disappearance was connected with his investigation of Screamworld, but he knew that the police would not do anything unless he could dig up some substantial evidence.

Not for the first time, Brent wished that he had an assistant, someone he could send off to do research or a little surveillance. He had nearly got as far as advertising for one, but he was essentially a solitary man and had baulked at the idea. Now he was stuck with too many jobs to do at once. He really needed to check for news stories about Screamworld by going through newspapers at the library, but he also wanted to take a look at Scarvetti's house, find out about the injured man from last night and, if possible, get a list of the amusement park's current employees to be cross-checked with police records.

One way to make the tasks more manageable presented itself to Brent. If he could make the acquaintance of a local newspaper reporter, they might be able to inform him of any old stories and say if there had been any rumour about last night's accident. Until he had more information from Cavanagh, that seemed to be his best bet. He would set off for the city centre in the hope that the reporters of the *Gloucester Times* were a garrulous bunch.

★　★　★

The newspaper building was tucked away down a side street in the centre of the city. It took Brent a short time to explain his request to the receptionist, who listened to the first few sentences and then cut him off brusquely saying that he had better talk to a Mr Fuller. Grudgingly, she granted him admission, opening the door to the rest of the building and rattling off directions before leaving him to it. There was a long corridor with doors leading off at intervals. He counted off three on the right and then opened the fourth door. The room he entered contained over a dozen desks and stacks of papers, files and notebooks piled up on every available surface. People were busy typing, reading or chatting to each other. It looked like a hive of activity.

The only person who noticed Brent's entrance was a corpulent man with pouchy eyes and an air of genteel poverty. He took off his glasses. 'Can I be of assistance?'

'I'm looking for someone called Fuller,' Brent answered.

'Adrian!' the man called out. 'It would

appear that fame has come knocking at last. Don't forget us lowly hacks when you hit the big time.'

One of the men typing glanced up, amused resignation in his eyes. He looked to be in his early thirties and was dressed smartly, if not expensively, in a plain dark suit and green tie. 'I could live a thousand years and not forget you, Roland.' He got up and walked over to Brent. 'Don't mind him; he doesn't get out much. So, you're looking for me?'

'Your receptionist seemed to think you might be able to help me with some information,' Brent explained.

'I sometimes think she just picks one of us at random.' Fuller perched casually on the edge of the nearest desk. 'What is it you're interested in?'

'I'm hoping for some background on Screamworld and its owner, Marco Scarvetti. It's to do with an insurance claim.'

'Oh! Well, in that case, I really am your man.' Fuller's eyes lit up. 'Come and sit down.' He ushered Brent to his desk and dumped a heap of files out of a nearby chair. 'Make yourself comfortable.'

'I take it you're interested in the place yourself?' Brent asked, sitting down.

Fuller nodded enthusiastically. 'It's a kind of obsession of mine, you could say. Old Roland there thinks I'm clutching at straws, but I'm convinced there's more to Screamworld than meets the eye.'

'Then I've certainly come to the right place,' said Brent, pleased that he seemed to be getting somewhere. 'The firm of insurers I represent are — '

'Is this about Gillian West?' Fuller interrupted.

'Well . . . it's to do with her accident, yes.'

'It was a bloody disgrace that she got hurt, but she could be considered one of the lucky ones,' Fuller said meaningfully.

'Lucky ones? Would you care to elaborate?'

Fuller looked to one side and leaned forward a little in his chair, his words conspiratorial. 'So far I've only got a few leads to go on, but it could be big.' He looked intently at Brent. 'You must have some kind of dirt on Scarvetti to have turned up here. Will you share it with me?'

Brent considered quickly. It was unlikely that it could rebound on Cavanagh Insurance if Scarvetti was a crook. Any malpractice would in fact invalidate the policy. The priority in any case was to find out if McAlister had come to harm. 'Yes, up to a point. There's some police involvement, and they might not appreciate me giving too much away.'

'Fine,' Fuller said eagerly. 'I can respect that.'

'Okay. After Miss West was injured, the insurers who cover Screamworld sent down one of their investigators, one of their best investigators. He was not satisfied that the company had been following all the safety procedures and said he'd be doing a thorough inspection. He disappeared shortly after. Now, it may have nothing to do with the park, or Scarvetti, but the timing is certainly suspicious, and I've been brought in to do some discreet digging.'

'Well, there's a coincidence.' Fuller started rummaging through his files. 'It's here somewhere, just bear with me.' A moment later he pulled a notebook, its pages secured by an elastic band, out of the pile. 'This is something I've been working on for months. Did you know that two local men have also vanished this year? Both were vagrants living on the streets in Gloucester, and one of them certainly had a connection with Scream-world.'

'I had no idea,' Brent said cautiously, unsure as to where the conversation was going.

'The police have done nothing at all to follow it up, perhaps because both the missing men are tramps.' Removing the elastic band, Fuller flipped through the notebook. 'The basic facts are here. 'Thomas Harper, mid-forties, originally from Swansea. Last seen in February of this year, in decent health and spirits. Kevin Barnes, twenties or thereabouts, beggar and sometime thief, last seen in early June.'' He looked up from his notes. 'Of course, a fair number of vagrants do go missing each year for various reasons, usually death, but sometimes they just move on without telling anyone. There was something different about these two, though; something they had in common. Look at this.' He removed a card from the notebook and handed it over.

It read: SCREAMWORLD. VIP PASS. ADMIT ONE. FREE FOOD AND DRINK.

Fuller continued, 'I got that from a tramp who sleeps outside a bookie's near my flat. I give Ned copies of the paper and he tells me any gossip he hears. Most of it's useless, but I've had a couple of good stories come my way through him. In March, Ned started asking me to help find a pal of his who'd gone missing. Apparently his friend, Tom Harper, had a very fixed routine. He begged outside the library during the day, and if he got moved on from there he either went to a spot near Woolworths or a lane by the cathedral. At the end of each day, he'd meet Ned and a few others to share a few cans before finding somewhere for the night. He was a bit simple, a half-wit who tended to trust people too much; and he'd recently been talking about 'a nice man' who'd given him 'a whole pound note' and said he could spot him a meal at the fair. When he hadn't turned up for their drinking session three nights in a row, Ned got worried and had me check the hospitals, thinking his friend had been taken ill. Well, I couldn't turn anything up with them, so I asked the police. To say they weren't interested is an understatement. Some bored desk sergeant took down the details and said they'd look into it, but nothing happened, despite me badgering them.'

'Do you think they were prejudiced?' Brent asked.

'You bet. Harper was a nobody, and they didn't give a damn. Then came the disappearance of Kevin Barnes. He was a different type from Harper — young, sharp, and with a leaning towards criminality. He was only on the streets temporarily; 'between jobs' is how he put it. He liked to work for someone else, mostly as a burglar. From all accounts, he was a slim, fit lad, good at going up drainpipes and through windows. When Ned told me about him, I must admit I thought that he'd either been nicked or killed. But then Ned started gabbling on about Screamworld. He was getting really worked up, saying that he'd heard things. Barnes had been boasting that he'd been given a freebie. He'd said he was going on a night out, 'courtesy of Marco Scarvetti'.'

'He used those words?' Brent asked interestedly.

'Repeated them several times, so the others say. No one's seen him since. Ned knows that a couple of local thieves have come round asking about him, wanting him for a job. They said they didn't know anything about his disappearance.'

'Any family? It sounds like he wasn't your classic tramp.'

'None that Ned had heard of and none that I could trace.' Fuller retrieved the VIP pass from Brent and turned it over in his fingers. 'I'm sure this is the key to it. We asked around, Ned and me, among the other vagrants, and quite a few of them said they'd seen a man watching them.' He flicked through his notebook, turning over page after page of shorthand. 'One of the tramps, 'Skinny' Hughes, put it the best. He told me that a man followed him around for a day. He wasn't there all the time but kept on turning up at the end of whatever street Hughes was in or in a shop nearby. By the evening, he was getting sick of the sight of him, but then the man came over and presented him with a pound note and this card, telling him, 'If you want a break from this, and a good meal, bring that to Screamworld. A free lift will be provided.''

'So why didn't he go?' Brent asked. 'I would've thought any of them would jump at the chance.'

'Hughes is scared of his own shadow,' Fuller said. 'There's no way he'd have gone there, unlike Barnes, who was a cocky young chancer; and, if I'm correct, Harper, who was easily influenced. Hughes held on to the card, thinking it could be a bargaining chip with one of his mates; but after Barnes went missing, he took fright and wanted to get rid of it. Ned got hold of it and gave it to me.' He looked down at the card and some of the excitement seemed to leech out of him. 'They expect me to put it all right, Ned especially. As if I'm some kind of superhero reporter.'

'That's a bit of a tall order,' Brent agreed. He was feeling distinctly overwhelmed himself. 'I don't suppose this could all be coincidence? Maybe Scarvetti has a charitable streak and the disappearances are not connected.' Even as he said it, it sounded weak.

'That's what my editor thinks. He won't stick his neck out on this unless I can get much more to back it up. That's why it makes a real difference that someone of importance has gone missing, your colleague I mean. It shouldn't matter, but it does. I just don't know where to go from here.'

Brent nodded, his mind going over his own plans. 'Last night there was another accident at Screamworld. A man, I'd say about forty, staggered off The Horror, looking like he'd been electrocuted. He was in a pretty bad way. The security guards, I think they were, took him off and he was sent to hospital. I'd very much like to find out what happened to him, but I don't have his name, and I was hoping you might be able to pull some strings on that front.'

'Good idea.' Fuller brightened. 'I know a few people at the hospital.' He put the VIP pass down, pulled a telephone close and dialled a number. When he got through, he asked for Amanda Corrigan and chatted for longer than Brent thought necessary before getting to the point. 'Mandy, I'm following up an accident that happened last night over at Screamworld. Can you find out who got admitted at about half-past nine, ten o'clock? It'd be a man, about forty. No, I don't know the name.' The reporter fell silent, obviously waiting for the woman to check. Then he sat up straight in his chair. 'What, there's nothing . . . ? No, I understand. Okay, thanks anyway. I owe you a drink.' He rung off and immediately started dialling another number. 'She's adamant that there were no men at all admitted last night.'

'I suppose it's vaguely possible that he was only treated in accident and emergency,' Brent said dubiously.

'There's more. Mandy asked one of the ambulance men if they'd been out to Screamworld. He'd just come off the night shift and scrounged a cup of tea. He said there was no callout there last night. Now, it could be that an ambulance was sent out from Cheltenham instead; and if so, Cheryl should know about it.' Fuller tapped the telephone to indicate that was who he was calling.

Brent thought back to the previous evening, going over what exactly he had witnessed. The 'long-coats', as he thought of them, had taken the man away and then the ambulance had arrived. Or, to be precise, he had heard a siren and seen a reflection of flashing lights from behind a boarded-off section of the park. He had not actually seen an ambulance.

He was not entirely surprised when Fuller finished his conversation and looked at him meaningfully. 'Well, that's strange. No ambulance was sent out from Cheltenham. Nor, would it appear, was any man admitted who fits the bill.'

4

The First Meeting

By one one o'clock that afternoon, in addition to having got what information he could from Fuller at the *Gloucester Times* offices, Brent had visited both the bed and breakfast McAlister had stayed at and the petrol station where he had last been officially sighted. He had learned nothing new, the accounts given merely corroborating what he had already been told and what was contained within Cavanagh's background notes. The information from the reporter was certainly worth pursuing, as was the mystery over the fate of the injured individual at the theme park. There seemed to be little doubt that something sinister was taking place at Screamworld.

'Is your food all right?'

Brent looked up and smiled at the young waitress. He had been temporarily lost in his own thoughts, so much so that he had barely touched his chicken soup. 'Very nice.' Straightening his napkin, he took several spoonfuls. Aside from an elderly couple seated a few tables away, the hotel dining room — a conservatory with wonderful views of the surrounding gardens — was empty of diners. He finished his soup quickly and headed for his room. Entering the main lobby, he was just about to start up the stairs when the receptionist called out from the main desk.

'Excuse me, Mr Brent!' The middle-aged woman beckoned him to the desk.

'Hello again. Has there been a message?'

'No. However, there was a gentleman in earlier asking for you.'

'Oh? Did he leave a name?' Brent was surprised.

'I'm afraid not, and . . . it was a bit peculiar, to tell you the truth.'

'In what way?'

'You see, this morning, a little after you'd gone out, a man came and asked about you. He said you were a colleague he'd met once or twice but he couldn't remember your name. It was all a bit vague. He described you perfectly, but I have to be honest, there was something about him that I didn't like. I'm pretty sure he was foreign.'

Brent felt a tinge of worry. Had he been followed from Screamworld last night?

'How strange! What did he look like?'

'Well, as I said, he didn't look or sound British. I did wonder if he was Italian, but that might have just been down to our conversation earlier. He was smart enough; dark hair slicked back, tie and jacket, olive skin, early forties. I told him that you'd be in later, around tea time, and that you'd booked in for a couple more nights.' The receptionist looked worried. 'I . . . I do hope I haven't said anything wrong.'

'No . . . of course not,' said Brent reassuringly. 'Did you actually tell him my name?'

'Why, no. I thought I probably shouldn't. We take our guests' privacy seriously.'

'I appreciate it. Now, if you'll excuse me.' Making his way upstairs, Brent's thoughts were a raging turmoil in his mind. Things had taken a decidedly unpleasant twist, and the idea that he was being shadowed set his nerves on edge. Going along the carpeted corridor, he warily approached his room, half-expecting the door to burst open and for some murderous assailant — an assassin hired by Scarvetti — to step out, a knife or a gun in their hand. Reaching the door, he unlocked it and stepped inside.

There were no signs of an intruder. Brent locked the door behind him. He sat down on the edge of the bed, pulled the phone towards him and dialled Cavanagh's office. Cavanagh's secretary took the call and immediately put him through to her boss.

'Well, John, how go things? Any new leads?'

'One or two interesting developments. It would appear that — ' Brent stopped at a sudden sound from the en suite bathroom. His eyes narrowed upon noticing a slight darkening under the lower edge of the door, suggestive of a shadow. 'Just hold on a moment.' Quietly he stood up, eyes panning futilely around the bedroom for something that could be used as a weapon. He listened, straining his ears, trying to detect the slightest sound. All was quiet. Mustering his courage, he made a dash for the bathroom door and violently flung it wide with enough force to knock back anyone who may have been lurking behind it.

With a loud crack, the door smashed into the tiled wall.

There was no one in the bathroom. Nor was there a window, so it was not as though someone could have made good their escape having been discovered. Savagely, Brent pulled the shower curtain aside to ensure no one was hiding behind it. Nothing. Looking down, he noticed that a towel had fallen from its hook. There was no doubt that was what he had heard. He took several deep breaths and returned to the phone. 'Sorry about that.'

'John . . . are you all right?'

'Yes. I guess I'm just a little on edge.' Brent explained the reasons why, informing Cavanagh about the missing tramps and the mysterious man who had come looking for him at the hotel.

'Look, I don't want you disappearing on me too,' Cavanagh said worriedly. 'If you think things are getting dangerous, then it's time you returned to London so that we can formally hand this over to the police.'

'You know as well as I that they won't do anything. They've shown no interest whatsoever in the missing tramps, and as far as they're concerned McAlister's jetted off somewhere with his bit on the side. Maybe I'm jumping to conclusions a bit early. As unlikely as it sounds, it could be that this person who's looking for me is completely innocent.'

'And . . . the man who was injured last night? Any further news regarding him?'

'I knew there was something else. Yes, apparently he too seems to have disappeared.'

'You're joking, right?'

'No. He wasn't admitted to any of the local hospitals. To all intents and purposes, he's just vanished into thin air. Now, it could be that he made a miraculous recovery and didn't need hospital treatment after all; but given the nature of his injuries, I'd say that's unlikely.'

'I really don't like this, John. There's something very strange going on at that bloody funfair.'

'I agree. And you're paying me to find out exactly what that is.'

'Well, that's not strictly true,' Cavanagh corrected. 'I'm paying you to find out what happened to McAlister.'

'Which, as far as I'm concerned, amounts to the same thing.'

There was a moment's hesitation as Cavanagh framed his response. 'So what's your next move?'

From his jacket pocket, Brent removed the VIP pass which he had, with the help of a little piece of deft legerdemain, filched from right under Fuller's nose. 'I'm going to pay another visit to Screamworld. Only this time, I'll be going courtesy of Mr Scarvetti. I do believe there'll be a meal included. I just hope it's Italian. I've always had a fondness for pasta.'

★ ★ ★

Brent had waited in one of the small rooms just off the hotel lobby, his face screened by the newspaper he pretended to read. He had sat there for most of the afternoon, hoping that the enigmatic stranger who was looking for him would turn up.

Two hours passed and there was no sign. A look at his wristwatch told Brent that it was coming up on four o'clock, the time he had decided to set out for Screamworld. Returning the newspaper to its stand, he entered the lobby, gave the receptionist a friendly wave, and left the hotel. After a final check to ensure that he still had the VIP pass, he went over to his car, unlocked it and got inside. Turning the key in the ignition, he felt his usual sense of satisfaction as the engine purred into life, and was soon driving smoothly out of the hotel's grounds.

It was a good twenty minutes' drive to Screamworld. A couple of miles into the drive, Brent turned off the main road and took a narrower one that bypassed a few un-signposted villages. The road here was deserted, and he stepped on the accelerator, enjoying the sensation of speed. The afternoon had become seasonably hot, so he rolled down the window, relishing the chill, refreshing breeze.

Trees, bushes, and swaths of ploughed agricultural land swept past on either side; blurs of brown, verdant green and yellow. On his first visit to Screamworld, Brent had been surprised to find it in such a rural setting. A sign directed visitors from the main road to begin with, but after that it was an exercise in faith to follow the minor roads until at last the turning to the carpark became visible. Presumably the most popular time of day was early evening onwards, but even so, a fair number of cars had filled the spaces closest to the gate and a small crowd of young men was heading in.

Brent parked his car, worrying briefly that it stood out among the cheap and slightly battered vehicles. If he had been followed last night, it would have been easy to pick out his Jaguar from the rest. Some private investigators he knew took great pains to blend in, adopting disguises, false accents, and even hiring appropriate vehicles as necessary — anything that assisted their inconspicuousness. That had never appealed to him, but he had to admit he had never taken on a job as strange as this one. Still, there was nothing he could do about that now. VIP pass in hand, he locked up and walked confidently to the entrance. Once at the ticket booth, he casually slid the card over the counter without a word.

The ticket seller, a young man in an unconvincing Frankenstein's monster costume, stared at it in some confusion. 'Is there a problem?' Brent asked.

'Well, no, but . . . ' The 'monster' scratched uneasily at his neck, causing the glued-on bolt to fall off. He looked uncertainly at the private investigator, taking in the neat clothes, the expensive watch and the general air of solvency. 'Look, can you wait here a minute? I need to check this. It could be there's been a mix-up.' Taking the VIP pass, he hurriedly exited via a rear door.

Brent smiled to himself. He had thought something like this might happen. The ticket seller had obviously seen the VIP pass before, but from his reaction, it was clear it had only been presented by tramps.

As he waited for the 'monster' to return, a second young man — this one bandaged up as a mummy — turned up, took his seat in the admissions booth and began to idly flick through a comic.

It was ten minutes before the 'monster' returned, and when he did so it was with an older woman. She was smartly dressed, with not a hint of Halloween style, and she wore a pair of dark sunglasses. Her ash-blonde hair was pinned back off her face. Sensible shoes, pleated skirt ending below the knee, and a white silk blouse completed the impression of almost implacable professionalism.

Brent was momentarily thrown. For the first time in Screamworld, here was someone who seemed totally normal. Like certain murderesses he had read about, there was a cold, almost glacial attractiveness to her.

'Please, come this way.' The woman turned and walked off.

Brent complied as, without looking back to ensure he was following her, the woman led him through the park, always staying a few steps ahead and exuding an unmistakable air of unapproachability. He took the hint and stayed silent, instead watching the reaction of the various stall-holders to their progress. The Screamworld staff glanced at them and quickly became visibly busier, giving the distinct impression that, whoever she was, she was a strict taskmaster.

Within minutes, they arrived at an unmarked door at the rear of the funhouse. The woman took out a key and unlocked it, held the door open while Brent entered, and then re-locked it behind them.

'Why the security? Do people try to get in here?' Brent asked.

Without answering, the woman led Brent up a short flight of stairs and out onto an empty landing with three doors leading off it. A bare electric bulb hung from the ceiling. She knocked on the middle door then opened it.

Behind the plain, cheap door was a huge expensively furnished room. Plush red carpet underfoot spread like a sea of velvet. Large modern sofas surrounded a low marble table in the centre, and a futuristic chandelier hung from the ceiling. To one side of the room was a well-stocked bar, complete with elegant bar stools, while at the other there was a mini-cinema set up with curtains, screen and seating for a dozen or so. Virtually every available inch of wall space had been covered with images from Scarvetti's films: zombies crawled from graves beneath moonlit skies; slavering werewolves tore their hapless prey to pieces; terrified peasants looked up into the maws of hideous blood-encrusted monsters. Even the less gory pictures were unsettling. A procession of cowled monks walking along an arched corridor in a monastery would have been a standard image were it not for the trail of blood their robes left behind on the grey flagstones.

Brent stared openly at the scenes. He had got an idea of Scarvetti's work from Mellors but had not imagined anything quite like this. It took him a few moments to notice the man seated in a revolving chair by one of the large windows overlooking the theme park. The chair spun round.

Marco Scarvetti closely resembled the large painting of himself that hung over the funhouse. The gaunt, cadaverous features and sunken eyes had been slightly exaggerated for the billboard; but overall, the Sicilian film director did look like one of the undead. His dark suit, although easily the equal of Brent's level of tailoring, lent him a certain funereal aura; and when he rose arthritically from his chair, it was as though he were pulled upright by invisible wires under the control of a hidden puppeteer.

Removing her sunglasses, the woman stepped forward. 'Mr Scarvetti, may I present to you one of our lucky pass holders.'

'Please, do come in.' Despite being accented, Scarvetti's words were cold, precise and chilling. 'Make yourself comfortable.'

'Thanks,' Brent replied. He sat down on one of the sofas. Was it true that this man had filmed the brutal murder and subsequent devouring of his wife by bloodthirsty cannibals? The thought sent a shiver through him which he found hard to supress.

'A drink, perhaps?' Scarvetti asked.

'No thanks.'

'I take it you won't mind if I do?' Scarvetti turned to his female assistant.

'My usual, please, Eliza.' Woodenly, he went and sat down opposite the private investigator. 'Now, I must admit to a certain amount of surprise. Our lucky pass holders are usually people from a different level of society. You are a . . . businessman, perhaps?' he said, accepting the tiny glass of green liqueur handed to him by Eliza.

Brent had prepared a couple of scenarios, depending on what reception the VIP pass elicited. He had not really expected to be brought to see 'the great man' himself, but had decided to impersonate Fuller, the journalist, if the need arose. He crossed his legs, settling the crease of his trousers unhurriedly.

'May I just say how impressed I am by all that you've achieved here, Mr Scarvetti. Your funfair really is the talk of the town, as the saying goes, and I believe it's a real asset to the local economy. I don't think anyone without your level of vision could have done so much in so short a space of time. Let me introduce myself. My name's Adrian Fuller, and I'm an independent reporter working for a subsidiary branch of *The Gloucester Herald*. We're a small newspaper; one that specialises in printing current stories, primarily local stories. My particular role is to present our readership with the social and economic difficulties being faced by many of our less affluent members of society and the steps being taken by benevolent individuals, such as yourself, towards improving their plight.' Noting what he took to be slight confusion on Scarvetti's face, he continued, making it up as he went.

'And whereas everyone knows of your talent in conveying fear and horror to the many, too few are aware of your charitable works. Take, for instance, your selfless distribution of your special admission passes to the homeless and the starving. Had one not fortuitously come into my possession, the identity of this great benefactor might have remained a mystery. And what a pity that would've been. Your deeds of generosity would have gone, not unappreciated, for I'm sure those who receive them benefit greatly, but definitely unsung.'

Scarvetti considered Brent, nodding slightly to himself. Finally he gave a low whistle and, like a man who had just escaped punishment for some misdemeanour, made a show of wiping his brow. 'And there was me thinking you'd be sent to get us closed down.'

'Closed down? Why . . . quite the opposite. We need more places like this and more people like you in our country.'

'I appreciate your sentiments,' Scarvetti replied. He took a sip from his drink and put it down on the marble table. 'Well, Mr Fuller, I'll let you into a little secret. Since I was very young, I've always believed in the importance of giving to those less fortunate than oneself. Maybe it is due to my Catholic upbringing. Maybe not. Certainly my mother always stressed the need to do good to others.' Waving a withered arm, he indicated the posters in the room and the fairground outside. 'Even with my films and with Screamworld, I have always sought to entertain in the only way I know and to the best of my ability. I'm sure you'd agree, wouldn't you, Eliza?'

Eliza nodded. 'Without doubt.' Unsmiling, she fixed her cold grey distrusting eyes on Brent.

'There's only so much one man can achieve, but what I can do is provide our less fortunate members of society with a hot meal and, if they so desire, an evening enjoying themselves on my attractions. I think it's important to give them that opportunity of freedom; that one chance to experience something outside their impoverished existence.' Scarvetti pointed at Brent, his wrinkled face creasing into an unpleasant caricature of a smile. 'I am glad you have come by my card honestly. I would hate to think you had stolen it from some poor mendicant on the street.'

'Mendicant?' Brent asked.

'A beggar, you understand? There are many where I was born like this. In America too. Your country is not quite so bad, but still, in every city they are a fact of life.' Scarvetti was clearly warming to his subject. 'Perhaps one day I will make a film about the problem. Why not? A documentary on the people capitalism has failed. I have a soft spot for communists, you see. Their imagery is so strong, so unbending. I take it you've seen *Battleship Potemkin* — the old silent movie about the Russian revolution?'

Brent shook his head. 'I . . . can't say that I have.'

'No? Well maybe you should. It is the best film of its kind. Without a doubt. It was utterly fearless. I saw it as a young man and it lit a fire within me. Not to be a communist, you understand, but to be a film-maker. The emotion Eisenstein put on screen was the only thing I had ever seen that felt true to me.' Scarvetti's eyes were bright, as if he had a fever, and he clutched an arm of the sofa. 'I knew that it was my destiny to capture the most extreme experiences of life; to shake people out of their cosy, ignorant ideas. Most men sleepwalk through life, only half-aware of their own existence. They need to wake up!' He almost shouted his words, as if they were a battle cry.

'Are you still making films?' Brent asked lamely. The Italian was beginning to worry him.

'Not at the moment.' Scarvetti relaxed

a little. 'Screamworld is my current passion. Maybe one day I will return to movies, when I feel inspired; but the promoters are a timid lot. They no longer have the stomach for my work.'

Brent could not blame them. 'So, is that what brought you to England? To have a change from film-making?'

'Yes. I decided to have a break for a few years.' Scarvetti waved his hand dismissively. 'I wanted to pursue my art in a different way.' He suddenly seemed restless and he stood up, not without some difficulty. 'Come over here,' he commanded, walking to the large window overlooking the park.

Rising from the sofa, Brent moved to the window and looked out. Judging from the view, he guessed they were level with the funhouse billboard. Groups of people were lining up for the various rides and the atmosphere looked friendly, if a little raucous.

'See! These people are alive! You can feel the energy from here. You must have noticed that last night.' Scarvetti gave Brent a sidelong glance.

For a moment, Brent felt panic welling up inside him. Was it one of Scarvetti's lackeys who had followed him to the hotel? Was the Italian cleverly and insidiously leading him along, well aware that he was lying through his teeth? Then he remembered that the receptionist had refused to give his name. There was no way Scarvetti could know that he was John Brent, not Adrian Fuller. Fuller had said himself that he had never visited Screamworld and had not contacted Scarvetti, as he wanted to gather more evidence. He had to hope that the other had spoken true.

He forced himself to ignore his racing heart and said with a tone of mild surprise, 'You're right, I was here yesterday. How did you know that?'

'A lucky guess! There was an incident. Some poor man was injured. Thankfully my staff are highly skilled in all forms of medical assistance. When my head of customer service told me of this, he also said there was a well-dressed man who tried to help. He particularly remembered as this man was not our usual type of customer, and the description matches you perfectly.' Scarvetti smiled. 'I appreciate your concern for your fellow human beings, Mr Fuller. A most commendable trait.'

'Is the man all right?' Brent asked.

'He's fine.' Scarvetti smiled. 'Apparently he had won a bag of firecrackers which he foolishly decided to let off on one of my rides. One of my men escorted him home after they had patched him up. It looked worse than it was, and I believe he's making a full recovery.'

Brent assessed Scarvetti's tone of voice and his body language, weighing up the fairly plausible explanation, but his instinct told him the park owner was lying. However, there was nothing to be gained from calling him out at the moment, and everything to lose. 'I'm glad to hear it. The poor man looked terrible.'

'The greatest pity was the fact that he failed to fully appreciate my greatest ride,' Scarvetti said. 'The Horror. It's a true wonder. You should try it.'

'I . . . I might get round to it,' Brent said insincerely.

'Excellent. Just what I had in mind.' Scarvetti turned away from the window. 'You can ride it with me. I'm allowed to jump the queue.'

'What, now?' Brent was surprised and not a little alarmed.

'No time like the present, and the VIP pass does entitle you to ride it.' Scarvetti put his empty glass down on the bar. 'Come, follow me.'

Eliza opened the door and stood to one side. Scarvetti had called the woman his assistant, but the way she handled herself was far more like a bodyguard.

Filing the thought away for now, Brent turned his mind to The Horror. At least if he was going on it with Scarvetti, the safety checks should be observed. Wondering just what he had let himself in for, he descended the stairs.

5

'The Horror'

'Now as I said, this . . . this is without doubt my favourite ride in the whole park.' Scarvetti ushered the private investigator towards The Horror, proudly presenting it to him. 'My pièce de résistance. You wouldn't believe the trouble I went to in order to achieve its perfection. It took years of planning, and even now I find myself inspired to make the occasional tweak as and where necessary.'

Hands in pockets, Brent took in the terror-ridden nightmarish imagery that adorned the ghost-train-like attraction. It was as gruesome as it was mind-boggling — depicting dreadful acts of murder, revolting mutilations, awesome creatures from beyond the grave, infernal devils tormenting the living, and things much worse. Everywhere he looked, he saw some new abomination; the grisly, phantasmagorical montage merging into an unholy madness-induced interpretation of hell on earth. In addition to the murals, there were many grotesque models: blood-spattered demons that bore strong similarities to the skeletal horned monstrosity which guarded the main entrance to Screamworld. Cracked ivy-covered statues lined the queuing area, their stone faces reminiscent of the more hideous gargoyles that perched atop the parapets of Notre Dame, frozen into bestial snarls.

'Scared?' Scarvetti moved forward. 'Trust me, it'll be an amazing experience. I'll go first.' He nodded to the vampire-costumed operator and, with some difficulty, crammed himself into the front single-seater car. He craned his neck, eyes on Brent as the private investigator reluctantly got into the small car behind. 'Believe me, you're going to hate every minute.'

Brent looked up, wondering if he had heard right. Then, to his alarm, a restraining bar fell tightly across his lap, wedging him firmly in place. There came a rhythmic clatter from the track, and then suddenly Scarvetti's car jerked forward. He gave a shrill laugh as it barged through a swing door that had a huge grinning skull emblazoned on it, and disappeared from view.

Brent pushed on the safety mechanism, checking it for himself. It hardly budged. He tried not to dwell on the horde of dark possibilities that impinged on his thoughts. Was this just an innocent, if unarguably strange, and indeed horrible, fairground attraction — something he would walk away from with nothing more serious than a numb backside from having to sit in the uncomfortable seat? Or was it something else? What horrors was he about to see once he passed through that door?

A few uneasy seconds passed. 'You ready?' Without waiting for an answer, the operator pressed a button on a control box on the wall and Brent's car stuttered forward.

The car struck the door and Brent tightened his grip on the restraining bar, unprepared for the wild movement. The door swung shut behind him, plunging him into absolute darkness. The car swung to the right, and a glow of light materialised — a flame atop a tall candle, which seemed to waver, the flickering glow now increasing noticeably. It then darkened again as the flame was blown out by an unknown agent. Within seconds, it was so dark that he could scarcely make out the surrounding walls; and the long guttering shadows in the corners were huge and black, filled with menace.

And then a leprous white emaciated thing appeared on a vertical rack. It was being stretched; elongated horribly, its limbs pulled to breaking point as though they were elastic. The thing screamed as, with an audible snap, the appendages were bloodily rent asunder.

The car swivelled on its axis, steering Brent forward, permitting him a close-up view; not that it was welcome. It then made an abrupt right turn, pitching him through another door and down an unexpected drop that took his breath away for a few seconds. With a soul-wrenching scream, a ghastly nine-foot-tall linen-swathed monster emerged from the shadows, one clawed hand reaching out. Brent's eyes widened with shock.

The hideous giant lumbered from the darkness. Its face was half-covered with ragged blood-soaked bandages, those parts visible green and mottled, scabrous and decayed. Drool leaked from a widening fang-filled maw. It raised a blood-spattered double-headed axe.

The car weaved to one side, then reversed backwards up the ramp. Reaching the top, it changed direction yet again. Breathing heavily, Brent saw the monster's frightening shadow edging up the ramp in pursuit. It was just a dummy; a mechanical model powered by wires and electricity, he told himself. Nothing more. He just had to remain composed. Keep everything in perspective. Tell himself that —

There came another scream from the shadows. Then a flash of light. Brent jumped upon seeing the withered being sitting in the car that had pulled up alongside him. He had watched *Doctor Who* once or twice on television, and this grotesque bore more than a passing resemblance to Davros, the malevolent rubber-faced creator of the Daleks. Hell glared at him out of a pair of deeply wrinkled eyes. Claw-like hands reached towards him. What looked like blood leaked from between its black lips. The thing cackled as its car spun off on a different track.

With a weak laugh, Brent tried to settle his nerves. This experience was certainly not for the faint-hearted. An instant later the lights dimmed, flicked out at the touch of a switch. Darkness and silence settled over everything like a dense black cloud, unmoving. For a long moment, nothing happened. Then, abruptly, Brent was aware of something dark and unseen that was moving just up ahead. He strained his eyes to try to make it out, but it refused to come into focus, to yield a definite outline so that he might recognise it.

There came another flash of light. 'Davros' — a grinning, evil thing of putrescent flesh, leered down at him from the darkness. Convulsively, Brent backed away in his seat, trying to control the strange thrill of terror in his mind. The muscles of his throat corded, pulled tight by the rising fear in him. Everything went dark again.

The car clattered on its rail, picked up speed and then, to Brent's complete surprise, it tilted to one side and did a full three-hundred-and-sixty-degree corkscrew loop. For the briefest of seconds he was upside down, crammed against the restraining bar. Then he was back on the level. 'Jesus Christ!' he exclaimed, his nerves afire.

With a crash, the car battered aside another door. A long, dark corridor stretched into the distance, the length distorted by curved mirrors. Along the walls were doors with small barred windows. The car slowed down and then stopped completely. Everything went dark, complete and utterly.

The thought that perhaps the ride had broken down and that he was now stuck inside this house of horrors filled Brent with a new level of fear. And then from somewhere behind him, out of the blackness, came a low bubbling murmur of sheer terror. Slowly it built itself up from a muted whisper to a loud groan, then into a shrill, piercing shriek of mortal fear that finally died away into a rattling moan. Ugly, drooling visages appeared at the windows. Some of the doors creaked open, and chain-festooned straitjacketed madmen staggered forth, gibbering as they came.

The car spun, went up a short ramp and entered another passage. Suddenly a ghastly child-sized figure, pale-skinned and vampire-like, dressed in a black funereal suit, popped up on a spring like a nightmarish jack-in-the-box. Such was the quality of its modelling that it really did look like a dead child. It swung forward, arms outstretched, its fang-filled mouth widening. A second figure sprang forward, its hideous face coming within inches of the car before swinging back. And then, just when Brent thought he was clear and about to enter another part of the ride, a third such monstrosity was ejected from the low ceiling. Its arms were spread wide as, bat-like, it swung upside down.

The rail dipped and the car went underneath it. Weird psychedelic strobe lighting illuminated the tunnel ahead. The walls, including the floor and the ceiling, were covered with large screens upon which dreadful snippets from Scarvetti's splatter films were projected. The tunnel was rotating, causing the images to spiral, creating a powerful hypnotic effect. Voices were wailing, screaming, crying — creating an unholy cacophony that chilled the blood.

The flashing scenes played on Brent's mind, psychically bombarding him with their incessant horror. He clapped his hands to his eyes in an attempt to shut out the terrifying images, but it was no use. Once seen, they continued to plague his brain as though implanted there, like retinal burn after viewing a glowing electric bulb filament or direct sunlight. Confusion and horror were uppermost in his mind, and he could not separate reality from illusion. It was frightful beyond all belief. Even his ardently sceptical nature could not fully dismiss this as nothing other than clever film trickery.

A clashing of reds and yellows that was utterly hideous beat at his eyes, searing right through into the core of his being.

Occasionally, something ghastly and horrible would leap forth and stare at him with crimson malignant eyes — something that had no face, not a human one at least; and he would shrink back involuntarily, until his shaking body could go no further. Desperately he tried to scream, to shout; to tell the ride operator to let him out. But no sound would come out of his mouth. It seemed to twist inward upon itself in his lungs to block the base of his throat, so that it was impossible to breathe properly. Sweat dampened his brow and ran into his eyes. How long the assault on his sanity went on, it was almost impossible to tell.

'Are you all right?'

Opening his eyes, Brent realised that, mercifully, the ride had finished and that he was back outside. He gazed up at Scarvetti. 'That was . . . quite an experience.' The safety bar had risen, and he clumsily rose from the car and got out. 'I guess I wasn't expecting something so — '

'Intense?' Scarvetti interrupted.

Brent nodded. He was struck by a momentary wave of dizziness that caused his surroundings to swim before his eyes. Squinting against the bright sunlight, he steadied himself against a nearby wall.

'Did you want to go on a second time?'

⋆ ⋆ ⋆

The Merry Monk was the first pub Brent had come to on his drive away from Screamworld. It was small and smoke-filled, even at that relatively early hour, and none too clean; but it sold strong liquor, and that was all that mattered to him. He downed the first shot of whisky in one go and ordered another, which he sipped more slowly. The familiar taste and warmth did something to counteract the shock of riding The Horror. He had left the park as soon as possible, foregoing the 'free meal' his VIP pass entitled him to, his only thought to ground himself in normality.

'I bet I can guess where you've just been.' The barman was watching his new customer with a mixture of amusement and sympathy. 'Screamworld. Am I right?'

'It's that obvious?' Brent asked, trying

to smile wryly but only managing a kind of grimace.

'You aren't the first I've had in here in need of a stiff drink after visiting that place. Hard men too, some of them, the type I usually have to throw out after they've had too many. I've seen them drink like they don't want to see tomorrow.'

'I can understand that. I wouldn't mind a bit of blissful oblivion right now.'

'I've never been myself,' the barman said. 'I can't say I'm much of a one for rollercoasters, screaming kids, or funfairs for that matter. And, after seeing what it does to grown men, I think I'm better off staying right here and pouring the drinks.'

'A wise decision.' Brent wondered about the advisability of asking for a third whisky. He decided against it and took the remainder of his drink and a packet of pork scratchings over to a table in the corner. The effects of The Horror were still strong within him, and he had to consciously fight in order to keep his mind focused on the images before his eyes, rather than those in his head. When he had got off the ride, Scarvetti had wanted to tell him in detail about the engineering and cinematic feats that had gone into its creation. He was clearly obsessed with it.

Trying to step back from his own feelings about the attraction, Brent could see that it was, in its way, a masterpiece. If terror and revulsion were what it sought to instil, then it succeeded admirably; and the fact that each person rode it alone was a stroke of genius. But why anyone would want to create such an experience was beyond him. He mentally shook himself. It was just a stupid ride and a distraction from his task. Or was it? Given his own reaction to the ride — that of a healthy and mentally sound individual — could it actually prove disastrous to someone weaker-willed? What about the man he had seen staggering away from The Horror last night? Had there been a firecracker incident as he had been told, or had the man just flipped? If he had tried to climb out of the car, to escape the horrors assailing his senses, he might easily have sustained injuries, and it would explain his look of terror.

Brent reviewed his progress with dissatisfaction. There was still not enough to take to the police. If he could find some real dirt on Scarvetti, they might take it seriously; but apart from the man being borderline certifiable, there was nothing tangible. The journalist, Fuller, suspected that someone in the Gloucestershire Constabulary was being paid to look the other way over the tramps, and that could be true. If would not be the first time Brent had come across corruption in the police. If that were the case, it would take incontrovertible evidence to make them look again at Screamworld. Evidence he did not have.

Frustration was replacing Brent's residual shock. He was instinctively certain that Scarvetti was both a liar and a madman. He was fairly sure that McAlister would have come to the same conclusion. The question remained as to whether the missing insurance investigator had found out more than was good for him.

* * *

It had just gone half-past seven when Brent stepped into the hotel. The lobby was empty and, unnoticed, he made his way upstairs and slipped into his room, relieved to see that everything appeared normal. The dreadful images he had seen on The Horror still played disturbingly on his mind, making him feel dizzy and nauseous; effects the whisky had failed to completely dispel. His mind was still spinning as he entered the bathroom and, running the cold tap, he began to splash water liberally over his face, relishing the refreshing coolness.

Breathing deeply, Brent gazed into the mirror, noting the tired, almost haunted look to his eyes. He leaned against the sink, felt for a moment as though he was about to vomit, then, unsteadily, he made his way over to the bed and sat down. After a few minutes, he had regained enough of his composure to reach for his notebook. Flicking through the pages, he found the entry he had made about Lionel Mellors. He reached for the phone and began dialling. It was picked up on the tenth ring.

'Hello?' a croaky voice answered.

'Good evening, Mr Mellors. I hope this isn't an inconvenient time to call. This is John Brent.'

'Who?'

'John Brent. We spoke the other day.'

'Why, yes. You wanted to know about Marco Scarvetti.'

'Yes. I was wondering if there's anything else you can tell me about him.'

'How long have you got?' Mellors said, coughing briefly. 'I daresay I've enough material for a sizeable tome on the man. That's if I ever get round to completing my work.' He broke off to cough at greater length. 'Excuse me, my chest is particularly bad this evening. Now, what exactly did you want to know?'

'Well . . . ' Brent paused, gathering his thoughts. 'I visited his theme park today and went on one of his rides, the effects of which I'm still suffering. Don't get me wrong — it's not just the dizziness or motion sickness, it's the nature of the ride itself.'

'Would that be The Horror by chance?'

'Yes. You know of it?' Brent was slightly surprised.

'Only by reputation. I've heard that the premise of the ride is based loosely on one of his less well-known films: *La*

Corruzione, or to give it its English title, *The Corruption*, It tells the story of a man, referred to only as Tito, who succeeds in driving his wife mad. It wasn't very well received at the time, although there was a certain Hitchcockian style to it that I personally think was underrated.' Mellors cleared his throat noisily.

'How does it play out? I mean, how does the husband drive her mad?'

'Various ways ... but the most inventive was by projecting films onto the bedroom ceiling on certain nights. Tito takes advantage of the fact that his wife has a history of nightmares and sleepwalking to make her believe that she's dreaming the horrors he's creating for her. He leaves bits of dead animals for her to find, ones that had been killed by an item belonging to her — a letter opener, or a silk stocking, that kind of thing. The purpose was to suggest that she had committed the acts herself. The scenes are quite surreal, the imagery almost nightmarish at times, and Scarvetti makes excellent use of light and shadow to heighten the macabre atmosphere.

'At the end of the film, the wife's attending mass, but when she opens her handbag to get money for the offering she finds a human hand in there alongside a bloody knife. The shock causes her to finally lose her mind, and she cuts her throat in church. We see her blood running through the cracks in the floor to the crypt below. The last scene is completely dark, but with the amplified sound of the drops hitting the cold stones. It's very chilling.'

'Sounds pretty warped to me.'

'That's Marco Scarvetti for you. So, tell me about the ride.'

Brent wondered how on earth to describe The Horror. 'Well, there's a section towards the end that sounds like the film on the ceiling, but it's really more of a total immersion in horror.'

'Ah, that would make sense!' Mellors exclaimed, and then had to cough loudly for a long time. 'Scarvetti complained in one of his rare interviews about the limitations of film. The fact that it's just one flat screen in a cinema — a place where people chatter, eat popcorn, smoke and canoodle. He briefly experimented with 3D but didn't particularly like it. If he's managed to create an environment where everything the viewer sees is under his control, then that would indeed be disturbing.'

'It certainly is!' Brent was finding it hard to keep calm while recollecting the ride. 'There were two things I wanted to ask you. The first is about that time when he was held in an asylum. What exactly was it that put him in there?'

'Apart from his entire back catalogue?' Mellors replied. 'Scarvetti has always been an unusual man, and he's played up his eccentricities to good effect, but something seems to have happened on the set of his last big film, *The Lazarus Cult*. It never got finished, and there were all sorts of rumours surrounding it, all unsubstantiated.'

'What kind of rumours?'

'The main one was that he had convinced himself of the existence of zombies. The film was going to be a semi-biblical epic about Lazarus, who the gospel of St

John tells us Jesus raised from the dead. Scarvetti took it literally and scripted a sword-and-sandal zombie extravaganza which claimed that Lazarus was the first zombie and the leader of a breakaway cult of Christians seeking eternal life on earth rather than in heaven.'

'Really?' Brent could not contain his incredulity. He had heard some outlandish beliefs in his day, but this . . .

'Truly. The film stank, of course. Only a few scenes were shot, at great expense, before the producer pulled the plug and got Scarvetti committed. The final straw came when he demanded a freshly dead corpse for use in the film and had to be dragged screaming from the producer's office, raving and blaspheming.'

'So he truly did go insane?'

'A temporary loss of sanity, at the very least. He had long been known as a maverick, but he had never put a film in jeopardy like that before. It took him just under four years to get out of the asylum, and I've heard that some pressure was brought to bear on the doctors to release him.'

'He certainly doesn't seem that normal to me. Not after what I've seen at Scream-world.' Brent considered how to word his second question. 'I think you said before that there was a certain air of criminality about Scarvetti's past. Can you tell me more about that?'

'Okay, but we're in the realms of fourth-hand gossip here. When I was researching him assiduously about ten years ago, I'd try to talk to anyone who had worked with him, no matter in what capacity. I found that those closest to him would pass on only pre-arranged versions of history.' Mellors broke off to cough harshly. It was a good minute before he resumed the conversation.

'After a while, I found out that the same phrases started to be used by my interviewees more frequently than you'd expect, until it became obvious that I'd find out nothing 'unscripted' from them. So I started to dig up people on the edges of his life — the gaffer's assistant, the catering staff, and so on. Well, they had some other stories to tell. It's widely known that Scarvetti is hard to work for, very capricious, very driven and highly demanding of his workforce; but what I was hearing put him in a different league. Anyone who disagreed with him more than once got fired, and he had physically attacked some of his employees for minor misdemeanours.

'A cameraman who worked on his 1966 hit film *Daddy, Why Won't It Die?* talked about a security guard who let an unauthorised member of the paparazzi sneak onto the set. Scarvetti found out and started thrashing the guard with a cane, screaming at him. The guard ran off, but was found dead at the bottom of a cliff a week later. He had driven off the road while drunk, but the rumours flew that Scarvetti had arranged for him to be killed. My source claimed that half the crew threatened to walk out and had to be paid extra to stay on.'

'Do you know if it was ever proved?' Brent asked.

'I never followed it up. My health started to go around that time. But I know a lot of people who would certainly believe it possible.'

'Yes, I can understand that. Thank you, Mr Mellors. You've been very helpful.' Brent prepared to finish the call. 'Can I just ask one final question, a more personal one?'

'Fire away!'

'Why on earth did you choose such a bizarre man to research?'

'Precisely because he *is* so bizarre! No one's done a biography of him, not one that got beneath the surface. I'd make a packet!' Mellors laugh turned into a hacking cough. 'Look, you may not like the genre, but Scarvetti was a great director, truly inspired at times. I happen to think that he got tipped over the edge and probably hasn't recovered. I doubt if he'll ever make another film, so Scream-world is now his whole world. I believe it to be a reflection of the man himself — disturbing, ghoulish, even terrifying.' He sighed. 'I'd love to see it.'

6

A Dangerous Encounter

An incessant ringing woke Brent from a disturbed sleep. It took him a moment to realise that it was not the telephone but the fire alarm. He turned on the bedside light and lay there, hoping that it would cut off, but it continued. Getting out of bed, he reluctantly yet efficiently slipped on his shoes, pulled his jacket on over his pyjamas, grabbed his briefcase and unlocked the bedroom door. He walked swiftly along the corridor to the fire exit, doors opening and worried faces peering out as he went past. A minute later, he was standing, shivering slightly, in the well-lit carpark with the other guests. Examining the hotel from the exterior, he half-expected to see black-grey smoke billowing from the downstairs windows, but there was nothing of the sort.

Finally a middle-aged man, presumably

the manager, appeared with the guest register. 'I'm terribly sorry, ladies and gentlemen. It would appear that we've had a false alarm, but unfortunately I can't let you back into the building until the fire service have checked everything over. I do hope you understand.'

There was a murmur of dissatisfaction from the assembled guests. One tall, lean and very annoyed man called out: 'Come on, Warren, we're freezing out here!' He was with a rather younger woman who Brent speculated wryly was probably not his wife.

'They should be here any moment. The station's not far,' Warren said.

'Not far? Who're you trying to kid?' voiced a sour-faced elderly woman. 'The nearest is in Gloucester, and that's miles away.'

'Please.' Warren raised his hands placatingly. 'They'll be here soon, I assure you.'

Brent yawned and checked his watch. It was several minutes to two o'clock, and in all honesty this was the last thing he needed. Rubbing tiredly at his eyes, he began wandering to his car, with the intention of waiting inside it.

The manager came after him. 'Excuse me, sir, but can you stay at the muster point? I need to do a roll-call to ensure everyone's accounted for.'

'Oh, of course.' Brent returned to the others, and the manager went through all their names and room numbers before checking his staff list. Each person answered with varying amounts of tiredness or annoyance in their voices.

Brent was surprised that there were so many. The hotel had not seemed to be very full, but there must have been about thirty-five people milling around. Most were single men, presumably businessmen, but there were a few elderly couples, one family and a handful of live-in staff.

The sound of approaching fire engines brought a small cheer from the gathered crowd, who were eager to get back into the warmth and return to their beds. When the fire engines arrived, the crew was quick to investigate the hotel thoroughly; but even so, it took another twenty minutes before the all-clear was given and the guests filed back in, some muttering darkly among themselves about compensation at having been needlessly awakened. The offer of a brandy from the manager won over a few of the discontents, but by and large most were more intent on getting back to sleep.

Brent was one of those who accepted the conciliatory drink, and he took it upstairs, locking the bedroom door once more. Sipping the brandy, he turned off the lights and stared out of the window, his suspicious mind running over the possibility that the spurious alarm was in some way connected with his investigation and perhaps with the mysterious visitor who had been asking about him. It took him a long time to get back to sleep.

★   ★   ★

Despite the disturbed night, Brent woke up feeling refreshed and energised. Nevertheless, he had slept later than he had intended, and it was already half-past ten once he had showered and made himself presentable. Going downstairs for breakfast, he recognised some of the bleary-eyed individuals from last night, greeting a few of them. Shared experiences, normally unpleasant ones, had a tendency to break the ice. The breakfast was especially good that morning, with several extras, no doubt laid on by the manager to compensate for the bad night. The devilled kidneys which accompanied the full English fry-up were especially appetising.

Warren himself was doing the rounds of the dining room, chatting to guests solicitously, almost fawning over them, ensuring all was well. Reaching Brent's table, he asked if there was anything else, anything at all, he could provide.

'I'm fine, thank you.'

'May I once again apologise for last night.'

'Think nothing of it,' Brent replied. 'Have you any idea what caused the false alarm yet?'

'Faulty wiring, it would seem, in the kitchen. The electrician can't come round until later, but it's all under control.'

'Not mice, I hope! I've heard they're

prone to chew through wires.'

'No, no. Of course not!' Warren glanced around, obviously hoping no one else had heard. 'I can assure you there are no rodents here. It was probably an inadvertent mistake by one of my staff. I'll know more when the electrician arrives, though God alone knows how much that'll cost me.' He smiled and left.

Whether or not he believed the explanation, Brent had already decided to check out. There was really nothing more he could accomplish on his own. He had met Scarvetti, reconnoitred Screamworld, including The Horror, and got some interesting but not conclusive leads on disappearances connected with the Italian. Overall, though, his investigations were proving fruitless. His plans were to return to London that afternoon, write up his findings and recommendations, present them to Cavanagh, and see how the other wanted to continue, if indeed he wanted to at all.

Finishing his breakfast, Brent left the dining room and went upstairs to pack and leave a brief message for Cavanagh. There was undoubtedly something strange going on at Screamworld, something possibly criminal, but what exactly it was, he could not ascertain. It galled him to admit defeat, but he was pragmatic enough to realise that he was stuck and that his options were limited. There really was little more for him to do. If Scarvetti was guilty and somehow behind the disappearances, it would be very hard, if not impossible, to prove.

There was a different woman on reception when he went to settle his bill, and Brent was pleased to note that the cost of the second night had been reduced 'due to inconvenience'. Placing the invoice in his briefcase, his attention was drawn to the hacking cough of someone just outside the main entrance. He turned as the doors opened and the familiar, if unexpected, figure of Lionel Mellors stepped forth. The film expert had smartened up a little and was wearing matching corduroy trousers and jacket and was sporting a tweed cap. In one hand, he carried a small case.

Brent was slightly taken aback but rallied quickly. Walking forward, he greeted Mellors cordially. 'I didn't expect to see you here, Mr Mellors,' he said.

Mellors straightened up from his bout of coughing and stared at Brent. His face broke into a smile. 'Surprised you, eh? Well, I suppose I've surprised myself too.'

'So . . . what are you doing here?' Brent asked curiously.

'Right now, dying for a cup of coffee. The train journey from Paddington was most tiring, and it took a while to find a taxi at Gloucester station. It's been over a year since I've left London, you know. As to why I'm here, I have you to thank for that.' Mellors set his case down by the reception desk. 'Just let me check in, and then do join me for some coffee.'

★　★　★

The coffee was good, though not as good as in Soho, Mellors opined. He had settled himself on one of the sofas in the lounge as soon as he had signed the hotel register. The lethargy that Brent had noticed at their first meeting was gone, although the man was clearly still in ill health.

'After our telephone call yesterday I couldn't settle my thoughts,' Mellors explained. 'Talking about Scarvetti with you seemed to re-ignite my curiosity about the world outside my flat, and I suddenly came to the realisation that it could be now or never.'

'How do you mean?' Brent asked.

'I'd been putting off visiting Scream-world ever since it opened, waiting for my health to improve; but I've no idea when, or even if, that will happen. I've long assumed that the final chapter of my book would be about Screamworld and how it fits into Scarvetti's body of work. It would be a huge omission if I failed to cover it, and I started wondering if it would even be there for much longer. The nature of your questions lead me to believe that the great man might be coming under official scrutiny.' Mellors stopped and raised an eyebrow questioningly.

Brent drank some of his coffee, considering how to answer the oblique question. He decided to ask one of his own: 'How did you happen to choose this hotel? I don't think I mentioned I was staying here.'

'No sinister methods, I assure you. When I reached Gloucester, I just asked my taxi driver for the best hotel nearest to the theme park. I admit, I hoped you might be here too, but that was merely a happy coincidence.'

None of Brent's reliable hunches were detecting a lie. Mellors was a transparent character, if a little eccentric. Although he was fascinated by Scarvetti, he was unlikely to be working with him. There was really no reason not to tell the other about his investigation. They were alone in the lounge, and far enough from the door that it would be hard for anyone to overhear. He quickly roughed out the facts and the suppositions to date. 'So there you have it. There may or may not be a reason for Cavanagh Ltd to suspect foul play. At the moment, I can't say either way with regards to either McAlister or the missing tramps. I personally dislike Scarvetti and think he could be capable of murder, but I can't get closer than that to the truth. Now, if Cavanagh decides to push further with the investigation, probably through Scotland Yard, then they might get to the bottom of it.'

'Can he do that?' Mellors sounded surprised.

Brent nodded. 'Cavanagh's well-connected, with friends in high places. He could certainly take our suspicions to a few men he knows. He really hoped I'd be able to find some hard evidence; but, as I said, I've nothing tangible.'

Mellors poured himself another cup of coffee, nibbled on a biscuit, and eased his back against the cushions. 'You know, of all the film directors I've studied, Scarvetti's the most likely to be both ruthless enough and clever enough to get away with murder. Most of the great film-makers get their emotions out on celluloid, and their private lives are, if not blameless, fairly normal. Yes, there are often affairs — but very little violence. When you're watching a Scarvetti, however, there's always the feeling, the frisson, that what you see is the tip of the iceberg.'

'I just don't understand why anyone

would really want to watch the kind of films you've described to me,' Brent admitted.

'I gathered that from our conversations,' Mellors answered with a wry smile. 'But an awful lot of people do value his work. He has a huge following in Europe and beyond, in his heyday, actors and writers lined up to work with him. Although he's always tended to stick with a relatively small group of people. He'd re-use many of his favourite actors and actresses in film after film. In fact, some of my colleagues complain that this weakened the impact of his vision. If you've seen the same actor tortured to death six times already, they argue, it's harder to invest in the character. I don't agree. Scarvetti drew different performances out of his actors each time, pushed them further than he could have with actors who were not familiar with his ways of working.' His voice had been getting rougher as he spoke, and he took a long sip of coffee before continuing.

'Take Carlotta Russo for instance. She appeared in a dozen or so of his films. Starting with a bit part, she soon became indispensable, and really seemed to understand what he was trying to achieve. Her depiction of an amoral demonic murderess in *The Succubus* was superb. She was in his last film, *The Lazarus Cult*, and I heard that she tried to stop his removal to the asylum. Sadly, she seems to have dropped out of sight since then. Probably doesn't want to work for anyone else. She could have worked in America; she had fluent English.'

'Okay, so some people rate him. What do you get from the films?' Brent asked curiously.

Mellors considered the question, then: 'I love cinema, always have done, and I've seen a vast amount of films. I've a particular fondness for costume drama, and I think you have to go a long way to beat Laurel and Hardy for humour. I wouldn't say Scarvetti was my favourite director, and he is undoubtedly gross and sadistic on many occasions, but he is a true visionary. I appreciate his unflinching pursuit of high emotion. Some directors of *gialli*, basically horror films, just settle for shocking the audience. Scarvetti wants to actually unhinge you. I suspect that he unhinged himself many years before his incarceration and that's why he's so convincing. If he is responsible for outright murder, then I imagine he'll instantly be declared insane once again and be back in a straitjacket. I have to say, it would be a fitting end to his career.'

'Well, I'll be glad to finish this investigation, even if it has turned out to be unsuccessful. I wish you luck with your book, though. You certainly have some sensational material.' Brent set his cup back on the saucer and stood up. 'I'll keep an eye out for it,' he said, and extended his hand.

Mellors shook the offered hand but held on to it for a moment. 'You're going back to London now, then?'

'Yes, I was just about to leave when you arrived.'

'I wonder if I could possibly impose on you.' Mellors looked hopefully up at Brent. 'I can get a taxi to bring me back, but I would be very grateful if you could give me a lift to Screamworld on your way home.'

Considering the amount of information that Mellors had freely given him, Brent felt he could not refuse.

★ ★ ★

Brent had seen the weather report that day on the television, forecasting that it was likely to be the hottest day of the year so far — a real scorcher — with the inevitable prediction of severe thunderstorms later in the evening. Wiping a sheen of sweat from his brow, he stood by his car, waiting impatiently, wondering what was taking Mellors so long. He looked at his watch, seeing that it had just passed midday. Now that he was eager to return to London, he was beginning to regret having offered the other a ride to Screamworld. Just what the film expert would make of the bizarre fairground was anyone's guess, but it had certainly not appealed to him. He was on the verge of re-entering the hotel in order to find out the cause of the delay when he heard an outburst of coughing.

Mellors emerged from the hotel. He

strode over. 'Sorry to keep you waiting,' he said, giving no explanation for his tardiness. He gazed admiringly at Brent's car. 'This yours?'

Brent nodded.

'Very nice. Very nice indeed. A John Steed car if ever I saw one.' Approvingly, Mellors ran his hand across the bonnet, then walked around the sleek silver vehicle, taking in every detail. 'Splendid gun-metal-grey metallic finish, black leather interior, very stylish one-piece wooden dashboard, twin aluminium petrol tanks . . . My guess would be that it's one of only a few dozen or so ever manufactured.'

'I'm glad you approve.'

'It must've set you back a pretty sum.'

'Actually, I stole it.'

'What?'

'Only joking.' Brent unlocked the car door. 'Anyway, shall we get going?' He climbed inside and got behind the steering wheel, opening the passenger door for Mellors. Turning out of the hotel carpark, they were soon driving through the pleasant countryside.

Brent drove for perhaps just over a mile

before they topped a low rise, then took the car down into a small patch of woodland. The trees closed in on either side. In places, the verdant canopy joined overhead; branches forming an impenetrable carpet of leaves which shut out the sunlight.

Within minutes, they came out of the shade of the forest into more open country. The car had excellent road-handling properties, in spite of the uneven nature of the surface in places, especially on the bends. Turning his head, Brent glanced back through the rear window, seeing the forest recede into the distance. The road which wound away behind them was still deserted — no, there was one car on it, far back in the distance, but coming up fast. A red car, he noticed; a bright, garish spot of colour against the otherwise green background.

It was approaching fast. Terribly fast. No one in their right mind would drive a car like that along this road unless they had a very good reason for it, or they were not caring whether they lived or died.

Brent applied a little pressure on the

accelerator, taking the speed up past fifty, then fifty-five miles per hour. 'Steady on,' said Mellors. 'We're not at the Grand Prix, you know.'

Knuckles whitening around the steering wheel, Brent kept his eyes on the rapidly approaching vehicle in the rear-view mirror. He applied more pressure on the accelerator pedal. 'There's an idiot driver behind me. Could be we're being followed.'

Mellors glanced back over his right shoulder. 'Trouble?' he asked quietly.

'It's possible.' With some alarm, Brent saw that the red car had almost caught up with them. Its speed must have been quite fantastic to have covered so much ground in so short a time. He tried to make out the faces of the two men inside, but the sunlight was glinting fiercely on the curved windscreen, and in the glare of eye-searing brilliance he could make out nothing. There was a tight, tensed-up feeling in the pit of his stomach.

There was a crossroads up ahead. The red car kept its distance. Briefly, Brent thought that perhaps he was doing whoever was in the red car an injustice. Maybe they were just a couple of men out for a quiet drive through this beautiful countryside, with no thought of violence in their heads. Intuition told him otherwise, however; an instinct that was to prove true when, with a sudden burst of speed, the red car pulled alongside, did a highly dangerous overtaking manoeuvre, and skidded to an abrupt halt.

A machine-gun was pointed from a rear window and a burst of shots were fired.

Mellors screamed.

Slamming on the brakes, Brent savagely spun the steering wheel to the right, throwing the car into a violent spin, taking it off the main route and into a narrow country road. Tyres bleated in protest as rubber burned.

Fire streamed from the red car's rear window as a second burst of automatic gunfire strafed the road with bullet holes. Mellors screamed a second time.

Brent took off like a bat out of hell. Strong sunlight shone directly in front, causing him to blink his eyes several times to adjust them to the glare. For a few seconds, there was a red haze dancing in front of his vision. Then he was able to see properly.

The round disc of the sun was in front of them now, shimmering in the cloudless blue-white of the heavens. Trees, bushes and swaths of open fields flashed past as the car reached seventy-five miles per hour. Behind them, there was no sign of the red car. Had they lost it somewhere along that twisting road, or just outdistanced it?

Realising that the immediate threat had subsided and that a greater danger lay in the prospect of meeting any oncoming traffic on this narrow road, Brent decided to slow down, his eyes constantly flicking to the rear-view mirror. His mind was decided. Once he got into a main town, he would report this attempt on his life to the police, having reached the conclusion that things had now got well and truly out of hand. That Scarvetti was behind all of this was, to his mind at least, a certainty.

Mellors was breathing heavily, his face the colour of chalk.

The red car reappeared, tearing up the

road in pursuit behind them. The gunman was leaning right out, his weapon at the ready. Tyres screaming, Brent spun the Jaguar round a sharp bend, almost lost control, then sped off along the straight again. There was a signpost by the side of the road, but it flashed past without him having any time to see what it was meant to indicate. A deft swing of the steering wheel and the car made a tight downward left turn.

'Have you any idea where the hell we're going?' Mellors asked.

'No, but I think we've lost — ' With a cry, Brent hit the brakes, swerving to the right to avoid a sleek black car which purposefully pulled out of a concealed entrance, no doubt in an attempt to intercept them. Desperately, exerting all of his strength, he sought to keep the Jaguar on the level. The edge of the road came up and spun beneath the churning wheels, and then they were flipping over on one side, sliding down a slope, soil and grass flying in a grey-green cloud. Two short slender-trunked saplings were instantly brushed aside as the bonnet ploughed into them, snapping them off at their bases. There was the first appalling crash as the car struck a tree stump, then bounced for several yards before hammering down in a stretch of soft earth.

A wheel hit a sharp rock. There followed a loud explosion of a bursting tyre and the car slewed round sharply, tilted and slid the remaining thirty feet with an ear-splitting screech of tortured metal.

Hands outstretched, Brent went forward. With an intense flash of searing pain, his head hit the edge of the dashboard. A dark wave of unconsciousness threatened to drag him under, but with a tremendous effort he struggled up from the black depths to see the sunlight glaring blindingly into his eyes. Somehow he heaved himself up into a sitting position. There was a redness to his vision, and several seconds elapsed before he realised that it was his own blood flowing from a gash across his forehead. He put his hand up to it and winced involuntarily as a stab of pain lanced through his skull from front to back.

Mellors groaned; an indicator that he was, at least, still alive.

Men were approaching, their voices becoming louder. Brent had no doubt that it was the occupants of the black car determined to finish the job, to make sure he was dead. He felt helpless, scared, believing this was the end. A darkness fell over him as his mind swam and he began to lose his grip on consciousness.

The men approached. One of them, a broad-shouldered, moustachioed hulk, peered in through the shattered windscreen, gave the wounded driver a cursory glance, then muttered something in Italian.

7

When Survival Relies on Deception

It was the slightly sweet, dry scent of hay that Brent first registered. It stole into his comatose mind as he began to wake. Keeping his eyes closed for the moment, he let his other senses return. There were low voices nearby, too quiet to be distinct, and he was propped in a sitting position, with his legs out in front of him. Distorted visions of the car chase were starting to come back — the flash of red in the distance, the black car swinging round in front of his and the sickening roll as his Jaguar flipped. The memory of the stunning impact as his head had hit the dashboard caused him to wince. He gingerly opened his eyes.

A large dim space swam into view: grey stone walls and old beams spanning the ceiling, fifteen or so feet up. It took a moment for Brent to realise that he was in a barn, leaning against a wall of hay bales, his hands bound uncomfortably behind his back. A sound to his right made him turn his head to look. Mellors was sat beside him, his face taut with worry. The film expert did not seem to have any obvious injuries, although he too was tied up.

'Thank God,' Mellors breathed quietly. 'I didn't know how badly you were hurt. Can you talk?'

'Yes.' Brent moistened his dry lips and tried to shift into a better position. He could make out three shapes, but they were standing in front of an open door, and the sunlight pouring in turned them into silhouettes. One of them held a machine-gun. 'What's going on?'

'Shortly after the car crashed, three men turned up and got us both out. I could walk, or rather limp, but you were out for the count. They flung us in their car and brought us here. It's just a barn in a field as far as I can tell.' Mellors stopped and was obviously trying hard not to cough.

'How long have I been unconscious?'

'Not long. Ten minutes, maybe twenty. I can't see my watch.'

'Who are they?'

'Italians, and I'm afraid that from what I can make out, they're 'connected', if you know what I mean.'

'Connected? You mean Mafia?' Brent asked incredulously.

'Seems like it. I understand Italian quite well. The small one in the leather jacket's in charge,' Mellors muttered. 'Christ, I think they've seen you're awake.'

The shorter of the three men came forwards. He was casually dressed in jeans and a dark leather jacket and cap. Dark eyes gleamed in his clean-shaven tanned face. He stopped a few feet away from them. 'Mr Brent. I'm glad to see you're awake at last. I was worried when your car flipped, in case we'd killed you. You shouldn't have taken off like that.' He spoke good English, with an Italian-American accent.

'When someone starts shooting at me, I'm afraid I'm not going to hang around,' Brent replied sarcastically.

'We were aiming for the tyres.' The Italian shrugged. 'I just wanted to talk with you.'

'Who are you, anyway? I suppose you work for Scarvetti.' Brent was trying his best to appear calm, but the situation was hardly a comfortable one.

'For Signor Scarvetti? No, I don't. With him, sometimes in the past. I'm Zucci. You may have heard of me.'

'Sorry, no. Should I have? You seem to know my name.'

'It took a little digging to find it out, but yes, I know you're John Brent, and I know that you've been sniffing around Screamworld, getting friendly with my old friend Marco.' Zucci moved closer. 'That's starting to worry some people, some very important people. People who you don't want to mess with.'

What the hell was he talking about? Brent thought furiously.

'I understand that you may not know Marco's history; not know what toes you're stepping on. So I'm here to explain a few things to you, man to man.' Zucci pulled over a bale and sat on it, looking completely at ease. 'Marco owes us a lot of money. Money for getting him out of the nuthouse, money for keeping his exploits quiet, money for making the police turn a blind eye, as well as money for building his Screamworld. He seems to have forgotten his payments recently, and that's not good. Not good at all.' Taking a notebook out of a pocket, he thumbed through the pages. 'February was the last time he paid. Can you believe that?'

'Where Scarvetti's concerned, I could believe a lot of things,' Brent answered, still trying to size up the situation. 'I'd like to know, however, why you wanted to speak to me so badly that you tried to kill us.'

Zucci threw his hands up in mock dismay. 'Kill you! I wouldn't do such a thing. Murder's bad for business. I told you, we were aiming for the tyres. How was I to know you had a Ferrari under the bonnet of that funny little English car? It's lucky Paulo was able to head you off.' He sighed. 'You should have just stopped. Never mind, we can have our talk now. It's very simple. Marco Scarvetti belongs to my boss, Lorenzo Carozza — body, soul and wallet. No little English mobster is going to take over.'

So that was it. Brent would have laughed if he was not in fear of his life. His snooping at the theme park had been noticed by more than just Scarvetti, and this Zucci had interpreted the suspicious behaviour according to his own world. Over the years he had been mistaken for many things, including a gigolo, but never a gangster. He was about to repudiate the assumption when, to his surprise, Mellors spoke up.

'You mean he's been lying to us?'

Zucci turned his attention to the film expert. 'Marco does that a lot. My guess is he's offered you the same deal he has with Carozza: a hefty percentage of the takings in return for your investment.'

'Something like that,' Mellors agreed sourly. 'He's been asking about protection too. We were hoping to pin him down to specifics after my colleague here had assessed the funfair.' He looked pensive. 'Do you mean Don Lorenzo? Head of the

Carozza family from Palermo?'

'The one and only.' Zucci was smiling again now. 'Seems like you know a bit about us, unlike your friend.'

'I've heard a great deal about your boss over the years. My friend here's a numbers man. He's only been with us a while. We sent him ahead to check out Scarvetti's finances.'

Brent could only listen and try not to look astonished. His companion sounded completely convincing, at least to him. He tried to work out why the film expert was portraying them as gangsters. Mellors had obviously heard of this Carozza before. Perhaps that explained it. Whatever the reason, he decided to play along with it.

Zucci was considering Mellors. He had made the assumption that Brent was the senior of his two captives but now he was forced to reassess things.

For his part, Mellors was looking annoyed rather than scared. 'Okay, Zucci. We were clearly misinformed. I hope you'll accept my sincere apologies for our intrusion.'

'I'll carry your apology back to Don Lorenzo,' Zucci said. 'He doesn't want any hassle here, just his percentage.' He turned to Brent. 'So, you're the numbers man? Is Screamworld doing well?'

'Yes . . . it's a highly lucrative business,' Brent invented.

'Why hasn't Marco just paid up then? That's what I want to know. Why did he think he could get your outfit involved when he hasn't honoured our agreement? Then again, Marco always was a bit *pazzo*, a bit crazy. Could be he's finally lost it. Maybe it's time we put someone else in charge, to protect the investment.' He stood up and looked uncertainly at his captives. 'The question is — what should I do with you?'

'You say that Scarvetti hasn't paid you since February?' Brent said hurriedly.

'That's right.'

Brent glanced at Mellors meaningfully. The film expert took the hint.

'Our organisation was only contacted two weeks ago. Nothing's been agreed, and I know my boss would never want to cross Don Lorenzo,' Mellors said. 'It was a regrettable mistake, but no disrespect was intended.'

Zucci still seemed to be making up his mind, presumably deciding whether to kill them out of hand or not. He lit a cigarette and distractedly flicked the lighter on and off.

Brent's heart was beating fast. If the mobster took it into his head to 'accidentally' drop the lighter, the hay bales would burn easily; and if they were in the middle of nowhere, it would be too late for them by the time help arrived. This place would become an inferno. The huge man by the barn door was enough to deter any escape attempts, let alone his friend with the machine-gun. Even if he tried to make a grab for Zucci, he had nothing to threaten him with. No gun, knife or deadly hand-to-hand combat skills to fall back on. He had always been good at his job, but it usually involved tracking fraudsters through ledgers and hidden accounts. He was not ex-army like some private investigators, and although he kept himself fit, he had never been in a life-or-death situation before.

Mellors was watching the Italian intently. When the silence seemed to get too much for him, he sighed loudly. 'Come on, Zucci, you can see that we're no threat to you alive. Let us go, and we can report back that Scarvetti is off limits. Kill us, and we become a problem. The — ' He spluttered. 'The last thing you want is a gangland war. You're the capo, you know how these things work.'

'Yeah, I do,' Zucci said blankly, his emotionless face somehow more frightening than any outright threat.

'Then you'll know that blood's a big expense. It could cost you your life.' Mellors spoke quietly, but his voice resounded with authority. Then he rattled off a phrase in Italian: '*Ben finisce chi considera il fine.*'

Zucci raised his eyebrows and laughed. 'I've never heard that outside of Sicily. Okay, I'll let you off this time. However, take this as a friendly warning. Scream-world's ours. I've got that place under twenty-four-hour surveillance. All I need is the order to move. If I see either of you there again, I'll kill you.' Leaving the threat hanging in the air, he sauntered out of the building, taking his two henchmen with him.

Once the sound of the departing car had died away, Brent turned his attention to freeing himself. With some effort, he managed to get to his feet. His limbs ached and there was a dull throb just above his eyes.

'I don't suppose you've got a penknife or anything in your pocket?' Mellors asked hopefully.

'I'm afraid not.' Brent looked around the barn for anything that might prove useful for cutting his bonds — a scythe or something else bladed. Staggering forward, he went to the exit to ensure that Zucci and his hoodlums had really left. There was no sign of their captors and nothing to see except for mile after mile of empty fields. The barn stood on its own, with only a dirt track winding off into the distance.

'Have they gone?' Mellors called, his voice cracking a little.

Brent turned. 'Yes. Now it's just a case of getting out of here. There must be something we can use to get rid of these bloody ropes.' He resumed his hunt and was finally rewarded with an old, yet serviceable, saw blade. Awkwardly wedging it in a crack in the wall, he made good use of the cutting edge, emancipating himself in seconds. Massaging his chafed wrists, he then pulled the saw free and cut Mellors's bonds.

'Well, I hadn't bargained on this when I set out from London!' Mellors exclaimed as he rose painfully to his feet.

'Really? By the sound of it, you're a hardened criminal. You're not related to anyone called Corleone, are you?' Brent asked, only half-joking.

'Hell, no! But I dare say I know my way around gangster movies better than most. I loved *The Godfather*, although I still haven't seen the second film. I had severe bronchitis when it was released.'

'You fooled me, anyway. All that stuff you came out with sounded genuine.'

'I meant it to. We were in serious danger, and we still are. I don't want to hang around here in case that thug changes his mind.' Mellors walked a little unsteadily to the barn door, where Brent joined him, looking out at the rolling green grass of the fields and woods all around them.

'Any idea where we are?'

'Very little. It was only a short ride in the car to get here, but I was squashed down on the back seat. I couldn't see anything.'

Brent scanned the horizon. There were several groups of trees, a river in the distance, and the farmer's track, but nothing helpful like a proper road. 'Christ knows which way we should go.'

'Perhaps we should follow the track,' Mellors suggested.

'I'm not sure I like the idea of that, seeing as Zucci could return that way. I'd rather just find somewhere with a phone and turn this whole mess over to the police.'

'Sounds good to me.' Mellors surveyed the undulating landscape. 'Is that a building over there?' he asked, pointing to the southern horizon.

Brent squinted in the direction. 'Possibly. It's a long way off, though.'

'Everywhere's a long way off from

here,' Mellors said, his voice resigned.

'Fair point. Okay, let's get moving, and you can fill me in on gangsters on the way.'

* * *

The heat had become oppressive, and the landscape, pleasant as it was, seemed endless. They had covered less than three miles, yet Mellors was finding it impossible to walk and talk at the same time, his lungs labouring at the effort. Wearily, he pointed to a small copse of trees a hundred or so yards away where he suggested they take a rest. Exhausted, his feet aching, he lowered himself onto an old tree stump with relief. 'I could really do with a drink. My throat's parched,' he said hoarsely.

'Yes, a cold pint would be welcome right now.' Brent scouted the area but found nothing to either alarm him or help them. Finding a decent grassy spot on the ground, he sat down. His face was painfully sunburnt. 'We should be safe here. I don't think we've left any tracks.'

He too was tired, but at least the fear he had felt earlier had worn off. He was shocked by how powerless he had been in the presence of a true criminal and, if truth be told, ashamed that it had been his companion who had got them out of the predicament. Now he wanted to know all he could about their situation. 'So what can you tell me about this Lorenzo Carozza?'

'He's old-fashioned Sicilian Cosa Nostra,' Mellors panted. He paused for a moment in order to catch his breath. 'I'd say he must be in his eighties by now, but still a force to be reckoned with. He has no problem with using violence to further his ambitions, but he does possess a certain amount of respect for the rules. He's been known to give people a second chance, but only once. If you cross him or fail him after that, you're dead. Plain and simple.'

'How do you know about him?'

'When I was researching Scarvetti's life, I spent a few months in Sicily. Stayed there from August to late November. It took me that long to make connections with some of the locals. I was hoping to find some stories about Scarvetti's youth.'

'So where does the Mafia come into the picture?' Brent asked, waving an arm to drive away a small swarm of irksome horseflies.

'The Mafia have been in pictures since the movie business started,' Mellors laughed wryly. 'They practically ran Hollywood at one time. As to where Carozza fits into Scarvetti's life, that too started early. Sometime between 1926 and 1930, Scarvetti decided to look up his uncle and discovered a shadowy world that would take him in, if he would accede to its tenets. Now, our young aspiring film-maker was interested in the influence that the Mafia had, but not so much that he was prepared to join them completely. From what I managed to discover, he did occasional nefarious deals with his uncle, who was a friend of Carozza.'

'So what about now?' Brent asked impatiently. 'From what Zucci said, Scarvetti's in trouble with this Carozza.'

'Very much so. I'd no idea that Screamworld was partially mob-funded, but if Scarvetti's been neglecting his payments, then he really must be mad. I felt rather bad about landing Scarvetti in it with my story, but to be honest, he's doomed anyway. I'd heard rumours that he'd held out on Carozza once before. There's no way he'll get away with it twice.'

The horseflies that were gathering round the two men were becoming unbearable. Brent was sick of batting them away and itching to keep moving, but he had another question to ask. 'Do you think that Mc-Alister could have fallen foul of Zucci?'

'I suppose that's a possibility. Zucci certainly noticed your presence at Scream-world. I wonder how.'

'Maybe one of those 'long-coats' Scarvetti employs was reporting back to him,' Brent suggested. There was also the bin-diving 'tramp' — Fred Haddow. Could he have been somehow involved? Perhaps he had been judging Scarvetti too harshly and the man was not behind the disappearances after all. He stood up, brushing off his clothes. 'Do you think you're ready to go on now? I'm being eaten alive by these blood-sucking insects.' Extending a hand, he helped Mellors to his feet.

They returned to the edge of the field and continued to follow the narrow path. Round the next bend, an even denser cloud of horseflies assailed them, clinging to their clothes and biting through the material wherever they could. The two men swatted angrily at the flying insects, and Brent tried to pick up speed but Mellors's limp was getting worse and he could only maintain a terribly pain-wracked trudge.

The day had now become uncomfortably hot and muggy, the humid conditions strength-sapping. Both men were weak, bitten and very thirsty, and each step had become painful. Brent had called several halts, at first to allow for Mellors to recover a little, or at least not collapse. After a while, he needed the rests himself. He began to curse the choice not to follow the track that Zucci had taken. If he had known it would take so long to get anywhere, he would have taken his chances with the trail, but he had expected to find some sign of civilisation much sooner. A city dweller by choice, he had never spent much time in the great outdoors and vowed never to do so again.

'I'm sorry but I must stop again,' Mellors said weakly. He slumped to the ground. 'I'm starting to wish I'd never heard of Scarvetti! I could have done a biography of Hitchcock or Sergio Leone instead.'

'And I'm sorry I ever set up as a private investigator,' Brent replied, sinking to the earth himself. A glance at his watch showed him it was nearly four o'clock. 'I was reasonably happy as an accountant, comparatively at least.'

'An accountant eh? So you're a numbers man after all. Although admittedly it can have an extra meaning in the Mafia — illegal lotteries and that kind of thing. What made you change career?'

'Boredom, I suppose.' Brent wiped his forehead carefully, avoiding the dried blood holding his cut closed. 'My family was very ordinary, very conventional, right up to the day my sister declared she was moving to San Francisco to join some flower-power movement. Our parents were hugely relieved when she came back a year later and married her childhood sweetheart, but I always thought she had the right idea. Not about hippies, but about getting away. It opened my eyes. I saved up for six months, then took off round Europe, doing work here and there.

'I was helping a business in Copenhagen with its accounts when I started to see discrepancies. Turned out that several of the staff were involved with defrauding the company. Once the authorities had cleared it all up, I was hooked. I read up on corporate law, fraud, tax evasion, anything like that, and I got work with a few investigative firms abroad before coming back to England and working for myself. It's well paid, I'm good at it, and it's never boring.'

'But you've never been in trouble like this before, I gather?' Mellors asked. He had his eyes closed and was leaning against a tree. His breathing had become laboured.

'Never. I've met plenty of crooks, but only white-collar criminals. People often have the wrong idea about private investigators. We're not all gum-chewing, gun-toting Humphrey Bogart lookalikes with a bottle of whisky in the desk and a soft spot for sultry dames. All of this business with the Mafia is way out of my league. It would have been too much for McAlister as well.'

They rested for twenty minutes; and then, after another thirty minutes' walk, they stopped once more in the shade of a small copse. Brent was beginning to wonder if he should leave Mellors somewhere out of sight and go on alone to get help. It was tempting, but he was worried that he would never find his way back. From the crest of the last rise, he had seen that the building they were heading for was a large house. He leaned back against an old fence post, trying to let his aching muscles relax. Footsore and weary, he longed for sleep. Looking round at Mellors, where he lay on the grass, he thought for one moment that the man was dead. He was incredibly still and his mouth was hanging slackly.

Mellors began to snore.

'Come on! Wake up!'

Mellors coughed and opened his eyes.

'It's getting late. We should get going.'

The break had helped, and they started to make good progress. However, the weather was changing. The oppressive heat was building, and dark clouds were starting to form, the bright sunshine having given way to a murky premature dusk. There was a heaviness in the air. It felt like a thunderstorm was looming, and Brent had no wish to be out in the open when it struck.

Mellors plodded onwards, his head down, concentrating on the rough ground as the first spits of rain began to fall. Brent was struggling with a blister on his right heel. His smart leather shoes had not been designed for this. He was flagging, the effort of putting one foot in front of the other becoming greater all the time. He stopped suddenly. Through the darkening gloom, he saw that they were now very close to the house — a big house, more of a stately home, walled off, with its own private driveway. The road that connected it to the outside world wound away through a dense forest.

The rain was becoming heavier. 'I don't

161

think I can go much further,' Mellors moaned.

'It's downhill from here. Another hundred yards.' Soaked, Brent staggered on. Wiping the rain from his eyes, he could now discern in better detail the large building they were approaching. It resembled a small castle, its walls crenelated. Lights shone in some of the upstairs windows.

Lightning threw a blue sheet of flame across the world, delineating the tall trees that lined either side of the approach to the perimeter wall. The dull rumble of thunder came a few seconds later.

The road lead to a large wrought-iron gate in the outer wall. As Brent neared, he saw the cruel-looking spikes atop the brickwork — a visible indicator that the owner took their security seriously; and then his heart skipped a beat when a second flash of lightning illuminated the words inscribed on the large stone plaque on the wall: Casa Degli Orrori.

8

A Terrible Discovery

From out of the darkness, two long-coated men had materialised as if by magic and had 'escorted' Brent and Mellors onto the premises. Looking round, the private investigator had seen that there were a few strategically positioned security cameras, so it was not much of a surprise that they had been picked up. As things currently stood, he was just glad to be getting out of the storm. What exactly they were now being led into remained to be seen, but for now even Scarvetti's 'house of horror' was a welcome refuge. That said, it was one weird place, perfectly in keeping with its owner's personality. There was a plethora of strange but beautifully carved marble statuary on the grounds. At first sight, his vision hampered by the darkness and the falling rain, Brent just registered the perfectly proportioned figures; but then he began to see a sacrilegious dichotomy in the art: seraphic figures were holding pitchforks, and winged demonic entities had halos above their horns. Further down the stone-paved drive were statues of beings who seemed to be a twisted conglomeration of both, all dramatically lit by the flashes of lightning.

The drive curved round until, through the lashing rain, Brent could see the main house and, even in a state of semi-collapse, he could not help but stare. Casa Degli Orrori was an impressive Gothic concoction of towers and battlements, crenulations and arched windows. Banks of thin chimneys topped the roofs, and gargoyles crouched at the corners of the gutters, rainwater spewing out of their mouths. Even though his knowledge of architecture was basic, Brent could see that the house had originally been a more modest Georgian affair. Presumably the romantic additions were down to Scarvetti.

The grand entrance was lit by an ornate lantern that illuminated the serpentine metal designs on the huge open double doors.

Brent and Mellors were ushered into a well-lit hallway with a grey stone floor. The room was spacious and awe-inspiring, with stags' heads decorating the walls and antiquated suits of plate mail positioned at certain points like lifeless guardians. A grandiose staircase twisted upwards to the floor above. Hanging from the ceiling was an ornate brass chandelier.

'Wait here,' one of the 'long-coats' said before entering a room on the left of the hallway. His companion took up his place by the main entrance, as if he were a sentry on duty. The two of them had said hardly a word since they had collected Brent and Mellors from the gate.

There was a stone bench near the front door, and Mellors sank down onto it appreciatively and closed his eyes. Brent stayed standing, and it was he who first saw the mistress of the house. A pair of sharp-heeled shoes sounded loudly on the stone stairs as she came into view. She had long, thick black hair and even features in a pale face, with dark red lips. A sultry dame, at last he thought wryly. Whether due to his surroundings or the woman herself, she reminded him of the seductive, curvaceous vamp from *Carry on Screaming*. Whatever the reason, he was just relieved not to be greeted by Scarvetti. Although he had been revising his opinion of the film-maker, he was very conscious that he, and in all likelihood the Sicilian, had been lying at their last meeting.

'Good evening,' the woman said. 'It's not often we get visitors. Did your car break down?'

As she neared, Brent saw that she was not as young as he had first supposed. Her eyes were so dark that the pupils were hardly discernible, and they had a look of hard-won experience. At least there did not appear to be two small puncture marks on her neck.

'I'm afraid that my friend and I got rather lost, and we were very lucky to find your house,' Bent said. He was standing in a small puddle as the rain dripped off him. What with the raging thunderstorm and this house, it felt as though he had just stepped into a bad Hammer Horror production. This might be the norm for

Transylvania, but certainly not rural Gloucestershire. 'If you've a telephone, I'd be very grateful if we could call a taxi.'

'That's no trouble. I'll see to it, but you must come and get dry.' The woman opened the door on their right. 'Does your friend need help?'

With some effort, Mellors opened his eyes and blinked a few times. His jaw dropped. 'Carlotta Russo! Good heavens! I . . . I never expected . . . I mean . . . It's an honour to meet you! The name's Lionel Mellors. I've seen every one of your films.' Feebly, he tried to rise to his feet, but such was his fatigue that he staggered and had to sit down again.

For her part, Carlotta gave a surprised smile. 'Well, I never expected to find an admirer out here. I've been out of the business for a while.'

'Once seen, never forgotten,' Mellors said fervently.

'Here, let me help you.' Gracefully, Carlotta slid an arm beneath Mellors's and, with Brent's assistance, took him into the drawing room. It was a large room with oak-panelled walls, decorated like an over-the-top version of every English castle Brent had seen in films. There were two stuffed bears, one each side of the unlit fireplace above which were a pair of crossed halberds. More suits of armour stood to attention at the four corners of the room, and a brightly coloured tapestry hung from the far wall. A selection of armchairs and a sofa were grouped facing a large television, and one chair was positioned full on to the screen.

Brent tried not to stare. If he had been asked to imagine Marco Scarvetti relaxing at home, he would have pictured the film director, troubled and pensive, sitting in a leather chair in a darkened study, a glass of red wine in hand, listening to some brooding, mournful, hauntingly classical music — Albinoni's *Adagio in G Minor* or something as equally neo-Baroque. He would never have expected to see Scarvetti eating a fish supper out of a newspaper and watching *Some Mother's Do 'Ave 'Em*.

'We have visitors, Marco,' Carlotta called out as she manoeuvred Mellors to an armchair.

Scarvetti looked round. 'Oh, hello again, Mr . . . ?'

Brent had a moment's panic when he could not remember the name he had given the day before. Then it returned to him. 'Fuller. Adrian Fuller.'

'Of course.' Getting to his feet, Scarvetti set his food on a side table and stretched forwards to turn the television volume down. 'I do love your British humour,' he said, gesturing to the screen. '*On the Buses. The Benny Hill Show. Steptoe and Son.* It's one of the reasons I moved here. Italian television is rubbish.' He sat down again, shuffling his chair around until he was facing them. 'But who is this poor gentleman? He looks half-dead.'

'Actually, he's a fan of your films. I was taking him to Screamworld when we had an accident; skidded off the road and then got lost.' Brent had made a split-second decision not to mention Zucci.

'Yes, Marco,' Carlotta said. 'Mr Mellors even recognised me!' Was it Brent's imagination, or was Carlotta conveying more than one message?

'A devotee indeed,' said Scarvetti.

Mellors was temporarily lost for words and just stared, awestruck. After all these years, he was now face to face with the man he had studied for so long. He could not quite tell whether he was in a dream or a nightmare.

'Quite some place you've got here,' Brent commented.

'It suffices. Fifteen bedrooms and an indoor swimming pool. As for the grounds, I'm not sure exactly how large, they are but I do have my own tennis court; not that I ever get round to using it. But please, come and sit down.' Scarvetti gestured to a nearby sofa, and both Brent and Mellors flumped down onto it. He turned to the film expert. 'Tell me, which of my films did you see first?'

Mellors's face reddened, and then he started to talk with huge enthusiasm.

Carlotta brought them all glasses of brandy and Brent sipped his slowly. He was wet and tired and somewhat confused. Scarvetti seemed far more normal in this domestic setting. Carlotta was a solicitous hostess and spoke almost perfect English, though with quite a discernible accent. The room was well-heated and the alcohol welcome.

Yet again, he found himself re-evaluating his opinion of the man. If Zucci had, in fact, been behind McAlister's disappearance, then his suspicions of the film-maker were unfounded. He shifted a cushion behind his back and felt like giving in to sleep. The miles they had painfully walked had taken their toll, as had the fear he had felt when he was in the barn. Part of him thought that he should warn Scarvetti that the Mafia were after him, and he cleared his throat to do so several times, but something held him back. Some part of him that was not exhausted and longing for bed. Some part that retained its suspicious nature.

Scarvetti was laughing. Brent realised that his mind had been wandering for a while. With a mental effort, he refocused his attention, aware that now was not the time or place to drift off. The brandy was making him even more tired, and what he needed right now was a strong black coffee.

From outside, the sounds of the storm

were increasing as it worsened. Lightning flashed, illuminating the grounds.

'Well, you certainly know my works, Mr Mellors. It's a pleasure to meet such a fan.' Scarvetti grinned broadly. Noticing the tired yet hungry way in which the film expert's eyes seemed drawn to the remains of the fish and chips, he turned to Carlotta. 'My dear, I think some food for our guests is in order. Would you kindly go and see what the cook can prepare? And don't forget to call for a taxi.'

'Certainly.' Carlotta smiled and left the room.

'Now.' Scarvetti brought his attention back to Mellors. 'Tell me what you thought of *The Unholy Triplets?* I was never quite happy with the ending of that one. I had terrible trouble shooting that. No matter what we did on set, it went wrong — equipment malfunctioned, there were one or two fairly major accidents, the animals we used were uncontrollable. Why, there was even talk of a curse. Additionally, it went way over budget; and as for the cast . . . well, they were drunk most of the time. That film was the reason I decided not to work with your English actor, Oliver Reed. Such an on-screen presence, and I'm certain he would have done some of my films justice, but it goes without saying that alcoholics in general are very difficult to work with.'

'Early on in your career you worked a lot with Bosco Marx, wasn't — ?' Mellors began.

'Bosco Marx! Now there's a name from the past.' Scarvetti laughed. 'He was without doubt one of the worst, if not *the* worst, film directors to ever stand behind a camera. The man had no style whatsoever. He lacked purpose and vision. Shortly before he shot himself, he got in touch with me asking if I'd like to collaborate on a sequel to my 1965 film *Daddy, Why Won't It Die?*'

'1966,' Mellors corrected.

Scarvetti thought for a moment. '1966? Are you sure?'

'Yes. Not wanting to sound impertinent, but *Daddy, Why Won't It Die?* was released in 1966. It came out the same year as Leone's *The Good, the Bad, and the Ugly*. I remember going to see both on the same day.'

Brent was only half-listening. A smile creased his face as he found his gaze drawn to the anarchic exploits of the beret-wearing Frank Spencer as the comedy drew to a close.

Carlotta returned a few minutes later with a generous plate of sandwiches: cheese and pickle, tuna and cucumber, and ham and mustard. 'I'm afraid I can't get through on the telephone. I can't even reach the operator. The storm must have damaged something.'

There was almost an air of inevitability about things, thought Brent as his heart sank. The last thing he wanted was to stay here any longer than was necessary, although he knew he could hardly ask his host to arrange for his driver to take them to Gloucester in this weather.

'Well that's settled then!' Scarvetti clapped his hands together decisively. 'You can both stay here until the morning. I'd be delighted to have you as my guests.' He waved away Brent's protests that they did not want to intrude.

'I won't hear another word. It's settled,' he said firmly.

★ ★ ★

Once all the sandwiches had been eaten and another two glasses of brandy shared, Scarvetti had insisted on escorting his guests to their rooms. It was clearly an excuse to show off his 'treasures'.

'Caligula! This must be the actual prop from the infamous *Sanguis Bibimus*!' Mellors exclaimed, trying to keep the horror, the revulsion and the awe out of his voice. 'Of all your films, Mr Scarvetti, this is the one that truly gave me nightmares. I couldn't sleep for days. A veritable masterpiece of modern horror in an ancient setting.'

'It's just a dummy,' Brent told him reassuringly. Yet, truth be told, he was not all that keen on it either.

The prop in question was life-sized, sitting on a throne, and contained within a thick wood and glass cabinet. The wax face was tilted back, mouth open, frozen in mid-laugh. There was an undeniable grotesqueness to it that was most unnerving, and the tufts of black hair that protruded from the sides of its head and grew from under the laurel wreath and crown it had rakishly perched on its head all leant a certain macabre, sinister quality to it. It wore an elaborate toga besmirched with red spatters. In one human-like hand it held a goblet aloft. Its overall appearance was as though it were presiding over a decadent orgy.

Brent had seen something like this once on television. For a few pence, that one had told fortunes. If this one did the same, he dreaded to know what terrible predictions it would make.

Scarvetti gave a knowing smile. 'He's far more than a mere dummy, let me assure you.' He lovingly stroked the outside of the protective case. 'He is the Mad Emperor. The Blood-Drinker! The Cannibal of Rome!'

The three of them were standing on the wide landing in the impressive hallway.

'You had it made specially for one of your films?' Brent asked conversationally. There was no denying the fact that Scarvetti was weird; some of the things he had already shown them amongst his bizarre collection of largely fairground memorabilia and freak-show exotica had bordered on the truly ghastly.

'Yes indeed. There were originally three. One was lost. One was used in the final film sequence — burnt to ashes. And the sole survivor sits here before you.' Scarvetti turned to Mellors. 'I bet you didn't know that just after *Sanguis Bibimus* was released, I started work on a documentary about the equally mad Emperor Elagabalus. A true . . . nutcase. Anyway, do you know about my wonderful props maker, Jacopo Weidenreich? He created this masterpiece and many others. The man's a genius when it comes to mechanisms. He worked with me on Screamworld as well. I'll take you there myself if you like, perhaps in the morning if the weather improves. But I can see you're very tired, and right now I think you should get some sleep.' He led them along a passageway and stopped outside an open doorway. 'This will be your room, Mr Mellors. I hope you find it comfortable.'

The room beyond was beautifully

furnished and gently lit. 'This is delightful. You're too kind,' Mellors said, stifling a yawn. He had clearly had the time of his life talking with Scarvetti, but the day had certainly taken its toll on him, and his cough was beginning to play up once more.

One of the men who seemed to serve the film director in whatever capacity was required, arrived holding a small tray with two mugs on it. 'Compliments of Signora Russo,' he said in heavily accented English.

Scarvetti took one of the mugs and handed it to Mellors. '*Cioccolatta calda*. Real Italian hot chocolate, not the watery stuff you get here. This'll send you to sleep. Not that you really need it. Good night, my friend.'

'Thank you.' Mellors took the offered drink and entered the bedroom.

Brent would have liked to have had a few words with the film expert alone, but Scarvetti closed the door and ushered him further along the corridor to a closed door on the other side.

'I've put you in here, Mr Fuller. I

thought you'd appreciate this room.' Scarvetti opened the door and switched on a light.

The room was small and windowless, with neat furnishings and a large bed over to one side. On the far wall was a large painting of a ruined cathedral amidst dark trees in a snowy landscape. It was so realistic that it took a moment for Brent to realise it was merely paint and canvas.

'It's good, isn't it?' Scarvetti said. 'Weidenreich painted it himself to provide a focus of attention. If you look closely, you can see satyr-like figures hidden in the ruins. If you've the time and the inclination, see if you can find all thirty-three of them. To date, I've managed to locate all but two.'

'It's very good. He's obviously a very talented man,' Brent said politely. All he wanted now was for Scarvetti to leave him on his own so that he could get some proper rest and try to make sense of the extraordinary day. He put his hand on the door and stood waiting to close it.

'Yes, indeed.'

'Well, thanks again, Mr Scarvetti, for

putting myself and my friend up for the night.'

'I wouldn't have had it any other way. Now, I bid you goodnight.'

Brent stepped forward. There was a faint click, and then the entire floor shifted beneath his feet, tipping him backwards. He felt a hand on his back, pushing him away; and then he was dropping, vanishing through the floor. His feet struck some kind of slide, and he went down on his back. 'Christ!' he yelled as at the last moment he managed to twist his body so that as he came flying from the chute into pitch darkness he landed side-on, thus saving himself from an even nastier landing.

His left arm, from the shoulder down to his elbow, bore the brunt of the impact, and the pain that shot through his body made him cry out loud. Skidding further along the hard stone floor, his feet collided with something, one foot slipping between what felt like the upright bars of a cage. With a groan, he forced himself to sit up. Massaging his damaged arm, he was relieved to find that it did not appear as though he had broken any bones, but had there been a light source he was pretty sure it would be scraped raw and bleeding. More worrying, however, was the fact that his foot was trapped. Try as he could, he was unable to free it. Panic threatened to consume him. In the stillness he could hear the sound of approaching footsteps.

A few seconds later, a sliver of light appeared, and then a door was opened. Silhouetted in the doorway were several figures. A light was switched on.

Brent blinked at the sudden illumination. With alarm, he realised he was in a cell, his shadowy dungeon-like surroundings segregated into four such cells, each separated by a short walkway. From where he lay on the floor, he could see Scarvetti and two of his flunkies.

Flanked by his goons, the film director moved closer, sipping nonchalantly from the mug of Italian hot chocolate.

'What the hell are you playing at?' Brent shouted.

Scarvetti stared at his captive with eyes now devoid of all geniality and hospitality. 'If there's one thing I truly detest, it's people who lie.' He took another sip. 'Now, tell me who you really are. I know you're not this Fuller character you pretend to be. I have my suspicions, but I want to know exactly who it is you're working for. Do this and I'll let you go. It really is that simple.'

'Any chance of helping me get up?' Brent asked.

'Of course.' Scarvetti gestured to one of his men to assist the private investigator. With an agonising twist that almost caused Brent to pass out and threatened to dislocate his ankle, the burly henchman forced the wedged foot back inside the cage. Clambering to his feet, Brent winced as a stab of discomfort wracked his body. Hobbling over to the bars, he reached out with his hands and supported his weight against them.

'Now then, let's start with your real name.' Scarvetti's eyes narrowed.

'My real name?'

'Yes. It's not a trick question.'

Brent's mind was working overtime, assessing countless scenarios whose outcomes were dependent on how he answered this question. If he were to lie again, come up with some fabrication or other, what good would it serve? Similarly, if he were to disclose his genuine identity and the reason behind his being there and the true nature of his investigation, how would that be received? That he was dealing with a disturbed psychotic individual was now evident. He gulped nervously, knowing that if he played his cards wrongly, the odds were he would not be leaving this cell alive.

'If you're one of Carozza's underlings — '

'I . . . I don't work for Carozza,' Brent interrupted. 'I don't know who that is.' Coming to the realisation that it would probably be best to distance himself from any of the murkiness that lay around underworld connections, he straightened, his grip on the bars tightening. 'My name's . . . John Brent. I'm a private investigator. I've been sent to look into the disappearance of James McAlister.'

'Then I'm pleased to say that you need look no further, for Mr McAlister's over there.' Scarvetti pointed to the cell diagonally across from Brent's. 'He's been my 'guest' for some time. He's either sleeping . . . or dead. I'll go and see.' Taking a key from a pocket, he headed over, unlocked the door and crouched down over a huddled form, which he proceeded to shake. 'James . . . you've a visitor.'

Brent's eyes widened as the prone figure stirred, sat up, and, with the Sicilian's aid, clambered to his feet. It was a pathetic scene, Scarvetti guiding McAlister as though he were a blind cripple, barely capable of putting one foot in front of the other. As the two came further into the light, his face creased with emotion upon seeing that the man he had been assigned to find was now nothing like the man he had known. For this shambling, sickly-looking, gaunt, grey-hued wreck of a human being appeared more dead than alive. The clothes he wore were unwashed and soiled, and there was a bad stink coming from him.

McAlister snatched feebly at something unseen, as though he were trying to catch an invisible moth, and began to whimper. It was obvious that something within his mind had snapped.

'As you can see, I've taken very good care of him,' Scarvetti said cruelly. He let McAlister slump back to the floor at the front of the cage and stepped outside, relocking the cell door.

'You bastard! What have you done to him?' Brent cried out.

Scarvetti smiled. 'I was hoping you'd ask.' He pulled a chair over to the side of Brent's cell and sat down. 'Listen, and I'll tell you.'

9

An Inherited Cruelty

The underground chamber looked old. Clearly it had been a wine cellar before being transformed into something far more sinister. Brent could see a few steps leading up to a door, which was currently guarded by one of Scarvetti's men. The four cells were modern stainless-steel constructions and were free-standing. No crumbling masonry to chip away at or dirt floor to tunnel under. Even if McAlister had been in good health, he would have been unable to escape. In his current state, even the thought was probably beyond him.

Scarvetti lounged comfortably in his chair, basking in his position of power. 'James here has helped in my research. A test subject, if you like. He's proved to be one of my most helpful . . . guinea pigs.'

'What the hell do you mean?' Brent

demanded, fear and hatred coursing through him.

'Ah, so you really don't know. I wondered if perhaps you'd caught on, but obviously not.' Scarvetti tapped the side of his mug absently. 'Where to begin?' he said to himself. 'At the beginning, I suppose. You may or may not know that I was thrown into a madhouse a few years ago. Some stupid, but unfortunately influential, people believed that I'd lost my mind and thought that I'd also lose their money. That, of course, was what really worried them. They'd have left me to rot in that asylum.

'Carlotta got me out. She set up a deal with an old friend, Lorenzo Carozza, head of the Palermo Mafia, to get me to a different country where I could be free. She understands me better than anyone ever has, even my son. He likes the family business, but he sees it more as a money machine. Well, it will certainly make him rich, but that's not my motivation. The Horror — in fact, the whole of Scream-world — is not about money. It's only ever been a means to an end. My life's been devoted to the art, or science perhaps, of instilling fear; of affecting people's minds, possibly even their souls. I achieved a lot through film, more than anyone else has, but the whole business is so stifling. The producers, the distributors, the businessmen . . . they all held me back. 'You can't do that! You can't do this! No one will ever pay to see it!' They just didn't get it. I had to leave the industry to fulfill my dreams.'

McAlister, still slumped in his cell, started to gibber insanely. There was a breathless, screeching cackle that changed into sobs.

'Ah, he might be approaching the next stage,' Scarvetti said, turning to scrutinise his 'guinea pig'. 'He's taken longer than all the others, which confirms my theories.'

'You're a monster!' Brent shouted. 'A murderer! What about the others? What about those poor sods you lured to Screamworld?'

'The beggars, you mean? Well, yes, they died but . . . I didn't actually kill them. They just couldn't take it. I believe it's all to do with the initial inner resilience of the individual; the robustness of the mind. My very first test subject ended up being merely a little strange following his participation. I think you've met him — Fred Haddow, his name is. Of course, he only tried the early prototype. My later efforts have been much more intense. You'll be pleased to know that I've improved the technique. Which is why I'm taking such good care of James, my latest test subject.' Scarvetti sighed mockingly. 'I can see you're judging me already. Such is my lot. You just wait. One day I'll be hailed as a visionary. Although admittedly, you may not be in any state to appreciate it.

'It's like this.' He fixed Brent with a disturbing gaze. 'The Horror was designed by me, with help from a few others like Jacopo who support my efforts, to break through the walls of the psyche. We're just like rats who don't see that they're in a maze. We scuttle along the paths, thinking we're free, though we are just repeating the same banal rituals day after day. I was lucky enough to see a world beyond the maze; a world without rules. Government, religion, the laws of society.' He listed them on his fingers. 'They all hold us back; force us to live as they want us to. I found that out back in Italy as a child, and I vowed then not to let them win. I wanted to tear it all down, to leave them howling in the dust; but I had no power then.

'For a while, I thought the Mafia would be my salvation, but they're as trapped by rules as the rest. Carozza and all the others want to recreate government with themselves at the head. All their petty little laws of 'honour' are ways to control us. Carozza thinks I'm just running a business here. A bizarre one, I'm sure he thinks, but just a business that he can milk for money.' He laughed. 'I stopped paying him months ago. He must be furious by now. I'm hoping he'll send someone to investigate. It's essential to my research that I get a — what do you call it here? A hard man? Yes, a hard man to test The Horror on.'

So Scarvetti actually *wanted* Zucci or someone like him to turn up? Brent was having trouble assimilating all of this. The situation was so ludicrous, yet so dangerous, that he did not know how to react. He almost expected Scarvetti to suddenly pull a lever or slide back a section of wall to reveal a studio with an audience, and tell him that it was all being filmed for some insane television show.

'You see, I'd only put men of weak will through The Horror to begin with, and they tended to crack too easily, so it was an absolute gift to me when James arrived. Oh, I know he was investigating the little incident involving that girl, quite unrelated to my experiments. But he turned out to be far more diligent than I had expected an insurance investigator to be, and he actually discovered the second track in The Horror — the special one.'

'What do you mean? There's more than one track?' Brent asked.

'Of course there is! The one you rode yesterday is the official track; the one that all but a select few get to see. It's track B that matters. Even a child could ride track A with only a few nightmares to show for it. When James was discovered poking around where he wasn't wanted, I decided to reward his inquisitiveness. Needless to say, he wasn't very grateful. They never are . . . except for Haddow, who as I said, is a bit strange. Admittedly, he screamed a lot at the time, but now he seems to have locked the memory away. He certainly keeps hanging around as if he likes Screamworld. I've yet to find someone who can truly benefit from the experience, but I live in hope.'

'You're even madder than I thought. How could anyone possibly benefit from being literally scared out of their wits?'

'Now that is the interesting part of my work! I know it can be done, because I haven't only seen it happen, but I've experienced it for myself.' Scarvetti's eyes gleamed. 'It was in a remote part of the Amazonian rainforest, a very remote part, that I tracked down the most enlightened people who exist on this planet. They undergo terrible trials as youngsters and have been broken yet made again. Made stronger. They can then see reality clearly. The monks who brought me up talked incessantly about the transformative value of pain. From the suffering of Christ on the cross to my suffering when they beat me. 'You should be thankful, Marco; we're purging the sin from you.' My blood still stains that cursed place of hypocrites, but they never wanted to help me, just to control me. The Catholic faith is an abomination, a blight on mankind. My final film, The Lazarus Cult, was going to be a nail in the Pope's coffin, but I was stopped from completing it. I abandoned any trust I had in the Church long ago, but I found the true way to salvation, and it does not need you to die first.'

Brent was momentarily glad of the bars that separated him from the madman.

'As I was already an adult, my trials had to be harder; and in the rainforest, they don't possess the technology to replicate horrors as I can. The dangers I faced were real, as was the terror and despair. Even so, it took one final scene to break through. The death scene.' Scarvetti paused and took a deep breath, his voice subsiding to a whisper. 'I regretted it, but their sacrifice was worth it.'

The story that Mellors had told Brent

seeped back into the private investigator's mind. The cannibals who had killed Scarvetti's wife and two members of his team. That had to be what he meant. 'You let them murder your wife?' he whispered.

'It was sadly necessary, but their deaths will never be forgotten. In fact, they form a vital part of The Horror.'

Feeling terribly sick, Brent turned away. He could hardly bear to even look at Scarvetti.

'All the people who have contributed to my vision will be remembered. I'm so close to perfecting the ride. You may even be the first to come out of it with your soul cleansed. You seem to be a more self-centred person than James here. I still think he might find his way out of the maze, but it's taking a while. He was a little too soft-hearted. Kept on crying for his wife. Which was quite useful, of course. Once I knew he was expected at home, I needed to find a reason to explain his absence. I couldn't very well send him back like this, could I?

'Luckily for me, Carlotta had been

staying in Oxford for a while — she's always wanted to be a student there, and living in the city was the next best thing. My son, Viscero, drove McAlister and his car over there, and she set up a false trail.' Scarvetti chuckled. 'Not perhaps her best performance, as she was rather hurried, but it worked. Of course, the fact that the investigating officer was rather attracted to her helped.'

'Karen Garstang,' Brent said numbly.

'Well done!' Scarvetti clapped his hands sarcastically. 'You found out more than I'd realised. Yes, Carlotta had wanted to live there incognito. There have been some awkward incidents with fans in the past. She was in just the right place at the right time, although we decided she ought to come back here for a while, in case any problems arose.' He got to his feet, pushing the chair back.

'I've a few things to organise before you can have your own private ride on The Horror, so I'll leave you and James to have a talk. So nice to catch up with old friends.' He looked at the drooling wreck that was James McAlister and giggled.

'Admittedly, the conversation might be a little one-sided.' Chuckling to himself, he left the cellar, ignoring Brent's curses.

★   ★   ★

The night wore on. At first, Brent had tried to engage McAlister, to reach whatever mental prison he was in; but the wretched man just cowered at the back of his cell, whimpering from time to time. When his family was mentioned, he reacted with such anguish that it would have been cruel to continue.

Brent was almost ready to give up; to sit silently in his cell and hope for some chance of escape later; but he had read somewhere that even people in a coma could often hear what was said to them and that it was widely believed to help. For the sake of McAlister, he kept on talking, thinking aloud. It was better than hearing the moans coming from the other cell.

'I've been a fool,' he muttered. 'I should never have allowed myself to be taken in by that Sicilian bastard. I knew he was a liar, and it's obvious that he's completely nuts. The others must be too, if they buy that rubbish he's spouting. Unless they've got their own plans, I suppose. Maybe the son humours his father as long as the cash keeps flowing in; and Carlotta's clearly besotted. God, I wish Mellors had never turned up! I'd be back home by now. Although I guess Zucci was going to follow my car in any case, and Mellors did get me out of that particular hole. I wonder if Zucci had anything to do with that fire alarm at the hotel? If so, I don't know what he hoped to achieve. Unless . . . of course, the roll call. The manager identified all of us when we were out in the car park.

'If Zucci was hiding somewhere, he'd have known who I was and also what car I drove. He might have thought that information was worth something. What the hell is Scarvetti going to do with Mellors? He's not down here, which is probably a good sign; but if I'm not supposed to come back from Scream-world, how can they safely let him go? Is there any way I can avoid getting put on

The Horror? Seeing what it's done to — '
He broke off.

McAlister had stopped groaning and was pulling himself unsteadily to the front of his cell.

'James?' Brent said uncertainly.

McAlister's face came into the dim illumination of the solitary light bulb in the room. His eyes were bloodshot, his face covered in scratches, and his skin an ashen grey. He curled his fingers round the bars of the cell door, and Brent saw that they were encrusted with blood. His mouth hung slackly and his lips were swollen. He whispered something unintelligible.

'I'm sorry, James. I can't hear you,' Brent said

McAlister licked his lips and tried again. 'Jhhhon? Is . . . it yoo, Jhhh — ?' There was a very faint glimmer of recognition in his eyes. It was small, almost infinitesimal, but there all the same. A sign that perhaps, with expert psychological help, some vestige of his sanity might be salvageable.

'Yes, it's me. John Brent. George

Cavanagh sent me to find you.'

'Khhhh . . . '

Brent leaned closer.

'Khhhh . . . illl hiiim. Khiil Scaaa — '

'Kill Scarvetti?'

McAlister nodded dumbly.

'I will. If I get the chance.'

With a final nod, McAlister retreated back into the shadows.

Brent fell silent after that. He kept going over his experience on The Horror; picking apart every bit of it, trying to debunk it all. He knew his sanity and probably his life depended on not succumbing to it. That track A, as Scarvetti had referred to it, had affected him was beyond doubt. What track B had in store for him, only time would tell.

* * *

Brent woke with a start. There were footsteps outside the door to the cellar. Shortly after, the door opened. A tall, slim-shouldered, dark-suited man in his late twenties descended the steps. There was an evil presence about him.

199

The stranger's features were those of a younger Scarvetti, and Brent realised that this must be Viscero, the film director's son. A pair of dark raven-like eyes flicked over the new captive uninterestedly. Viscero then turned to the gun-carrying 'long-coat' who had followed him into the cellar. 'Take him out and get him into the van,' he ordered, pointing to Brent. Maliciously, he wandered over to McAlister's cell and rattled the bars like an obnoxious child pestering the animals at the zoo. 'So you're not dead yet? Won't be long.'

Brent seethed. He had met this kind of playboy bully before: rich, callous, arrogant, and as self-centred as a gyroscope. Having Scarvetti as a father had probably added an edge of violence to the man as well. It really was a case of like father, like son. There would be no reasoning with this sick-minded individual.

The henchman unlocked the cage door and gestured for Brent to step outside. Aware that unless he were to make an escape bid, he could well end up effectively lobotomised like the unfortunate McAlister, Brent lunged for the gunman's arm, twisted it back and forced his assailant to drop the weapon. He then followed up with a swift kick to the 'long-coat's' shin, spun him around and, using all of his strength, flung him forward towards Scarvetti's son, who was desperately scrabbling for the gun. Viscero gave a muffled curse as Brent stepped forward and kicked the gun out of his reach.

The 'long-coat' had regained his footing. He lashed out with a savage punch that struck Brent a glancing blow on the jaw. It had been many years since the private investigator had been physically attacked — and that had only been a short-lived mugging attempt on the London Underground — so that for a moment he was more stunned than hurt. Then the pain registered, and he felt his senses slipping away as he almost collapsed. Somehow he manged to stay upright, and raised an arm to block another incoming punch. He felt lit with a sudden blaze of rage. Leaping forward, it was now his turn to smash a blow on the other's exposed chin. His knuckles smote the man's nose, bursting it and cracking the front upper teeth. Blood streamed from the 'long-coat's' mouth as he staggered back.

Viscero came at a rush, arms extended. A harsh roar came from his throat. He heaved upwards with a surge of super-human strength, caught Brent and carried him backwards, pinning him against a wall. Fingers then locked around the private investigator's throat.

Brent panicked. He felt his strength weakening against the stranglehold. He could not draw in a single breath. There was a pounding in his head — a gigantic sledgehammer thundering against the walls of his brain. He felt his tongue start to protrude from his parted lips; felt his eyeballs bulge as the tremendous pressure increased. His arms hung limply. Through blurred vision, he saw the other's grinning features; saw the look of diabolical triumph in the piercing, dark eyes.

A sudden gunshot rang out.

Viscero turned, his grip lessening.

Brent's reaction was purely instinctive. Taking advantage of the other's momentary distraction, he clenched his right fist and drove it into his attacker's ribs. In pain, Viscero squeezed his eyes shut, and the stranglehold on Brent's throat loosened.

There was a second shot, and then a third, followed by a scream.

Clutching his abdomen, the 'long-coat' staggered forward, blood streaming from his nose and from between his fingers. His eyes misted over, and he then sank to his knees before crumpling face first to the floor.

Over Viscero's shoulder, Brent could see that the incarcerated McAlister was now in possession of the gun, his arm wobbling unsteadily as he tried to take aim from between the cell bars.

Viscero cursed, broke his stranglehold and stepped back, ready to make a run for it. Gasping with pain, Brent made a furious snatch for him, grabbing hold of his dark suit. Fabric tore as he pulled savagely, hauling the younger Scarvetti towards him. He spun the man around, presenting McAlister with a good target. 'Shoot him!' he shouted.

Like an oiled snake, Viscero slid from Brent's hold and made a mad dash for the exit. McAlister fired twice, but both shots went wide.

Breathing heavily, Brent considered going in pursuit. His thoughts turned to McAlister, wondering if there was any way of rescuing him. He would have to be quick about it, for there was no doubt Viscero would return with reinforcements. Hastily he began searching for the keys to the cell. 'Hold on, James. I'll — ' He jumped at the final report from the gun. With a gulp, he spun round, his nerves afire.

McAlister had saved the final bullet for himself.

'No!' Brent cried. 'No!' He felt the strength leaving his legs. Stumbling to one side, his stomach lurched violently and he threw up. Clutching his head, he then backed away, oblivious to the three men who now stood in the doorway, two of whom were armed with handguns.

* * *

Brent was thrown forcibly to the floor of the van. His hands had been bound behind his back, making it impossible to stop his fall. Pulling his legs up, he managed to manoeuvre himself until he got his back against one of the sides. The sound of McAlister's final bullet still seemed to ring in his ears.

Viscero climbed in after him, sat down on a sturdy packing crate, and switched an interior light on. 'Not my preferred means of transport, but it's only a short journey.' He banged on the partition separating the back of the van from the driver. 'Okay, you can go!'

The van started up.

'The old man thinks that you'll survive The Horror, but you strike me as a loser. I'll enjoy watching you crack. There's a special viewing room and we record it all. The ride affects people in stages, from the seriously freaked out through to the blubbering insanity. In the early parts, your friend McAlister was still coherent enough to beg for release. The vagrants were useless. Even intoxicated, they broke almost immediately. My father treats it like some great experiment, as he's no doubt told you, and he insists that we document everything.'

'That's risky,' Brent said, working hard to get his swollen lips to move. 'If the paperwork was found, it would convict you all.'

'True. But it's going to make it very easy to market the system.' Viscero was examining the left cuff of his shirt. 'Damn! You got blood on it.' He gingerly felt the side of his face, which was rapidly bruising.

'Market the system?'

'To the KGB, China or North Korea in the first instance. The CIA are too weak to see the possibilities, and I know it's not the Mafia's style, but my preliminary talks with my contacts in the Soviet Union have been very encouraging.' Viscero noted Brent's look of dawning comprehension. 'You getting it now?'

'Psychological torture! You want to sell it as some kind of interrogation device?' Brent could see the possibilities all too clearly.

'Exactly. You can forget all that rubbish about 'setting people free from the maze'. That's just my father's obsession, and he won't last much longer. He's a liability these days. Has been ever since he left the asylum. I've been quietly taking over the business. All of security reports to me now, and they know the score. Eliza's ready to act on my word. Now that The Horror is perfected, for my purposes anyway, we're scrapping Screamworld. The old man's a genius at what he does, I won't deny that, but he takes too many chances; and of course he's completely insane. Only Carlotta and a couple of his old cronies are still loyal to him. I'll set them up somewhere, possibly a nice villa near the Black Sea, and he can slide into obscurity.'

Brent stared at Viscero with utter disgust. 'You're even worse than he is. At least he has the excuse of madness to explain his actions. You're just scum.'

'Obscenely wealthy scum,' Viscero corrected. 'Or at least I will be.' He looked at his watch. 'We'll have to be quick at Screamworld. I'm prepared to indulge my father one last time and let him put you through The Horror. I could use the extra footage anyway, but we need to get out of the country by morning. I took a very interesting telephone call earlier this evening from Scotland Yard. They've made an appointment to call on my father tomorrow to discuss certain 'irregularities'. Believe it or not, your name was mentioned.'

So Cavanagh had taken fright and called in his favours, Brent thought. Shame it was too late. He was starting to feel that his end was inevitable. With the film director in charge, he had hoped that there might be some way to avoid his fate, but Viscero was another proposition. It would take a minor miracle to save him now. His thoughts moved to Mellors, presumably still asleep back at Scarvetti's house. 'Will you at least let my friend go? He has no idea what's going on.'

Viscero shrugged boredly. 'He doesn't matter. We'll be long gone by the time he comes to. Carlotta's knock-out drugs always work. Unless he has a weak heart, in which case he may never wake up.'

A voice called from the front of the van, 'We're here, sir.'

'Good. Drive us right up to the entrance. I want to get this over with and go. Have you got the lorries in place?'

'Yes, sir. The crew's ready to dismantle the ride on your word and the ship's waiting in the Bristol Chanel.'

Viscero grinned nastily at Brent. 'Only one more detail to take care of, then. Are you ready for your close-up?'

10

A Fate Worse than Death

Kicking and screaming, manhandled by four of the 'long-coats', Brent was dragged like a sacrificial victim towards The Horror. His hands were still bound, but he fought fiercely, kicking, stamping, butting. One unfortunate 'heavy' received a powerful kick to the groin that sent him reeling.

'You'll never get away with this, you bastard!' Brent ranted.

'I will, you know,' Viscero replied calmly.

Cursing savagely, Brent was forced unceremoniously into the waiting car. It proved to be a painful manoeuvre. At Viscero's orders, the restraining bar was lowered. One of the 'long-coats' pushed it down even further, firmly wedging the private investigator into his seat.

'I guess it must be worse, knowing

what's to come,' Viscero said. 'Those others who've gone through had no idea of the effect it was going to have on them. They just saw this ride as another fairground attraction — a rather upmarket ghost train. Now, the old man said you've to go through exactly on two o'clock so that he can be in place to watch you on his monitors. That leaves you . . . ' He checked his wristwatch. ' . . . just under seven minutes. Normally I believe it traditional to offer the condemned man a last request.'

'Then drop dead,' Brent snarled.

'But who cares about tradition?' Viscero shrugged. 'You'll have to wear these, I'm afraid.' He drew a strangely modified pair of swimming goggles from a pocket. 'Not only do they give 3D vision, but they'll ensure you can't close your eyes. Not that I think you would, of course. It's the first time we've needed to use them, so they may be a little uncomfortable. My father's friend, Jacopo, got the idea from *A Clockwork Orange*. You may've seen it.'

Brent had indeed seen the film, and found it disturbing.

Viscero got two men to hold Brent's head still while he positioned the goggles so that the protruding plastic rings pulled the eyelids open, pinning them back. After adjusting them several times, he was finally satisfied. 'That looks about right,' he said. 'We don't want you to miss out on anything.' Stepping back, he looked around at Screamworld. The torrential rain had stopped, leaving a clear, starry night. The amusement park was empty and silent save for Viscero's men. 'I might actually miss this place, you know. It's so . . . unashamedly vulgar. Maybe I'll start up something similar wherever we end up.' He checked his watch once more. 'Nearly time for your starring role, Mr Brent. I'll be interested to see your performance.'

'I can pay you, if money's your motivation,' Brent said in desperation.

Viscero laughed. 'Not as much as the Kremlin can! You'd better just accept that your destiny has led you to this point. That you were always intended to end up here. Either that, or blind chance.' He gave one last tug at the security bar to check it was secure, then signalled to the ride operator. He gave Brent a condescending pat on the shoulder. 'Don't forget to smile for the cameras.'

A faint crackle of electricity ran along the track as it was powered up. Brent tensed.

The car, with its trapped occupant, started to move forward. It battered its way through the heavy swing door and into the interior of The Horror.

As soon as he was out of sight of Viscero, Brent started shaking his head violently, trying to free it from the restraining band, or at least dislodge the goggles. There was some give, but not enough to allow him to turn his head, and the weird spectacles seemed locked firmly in place. It was completely dark; and then, just like his previous experience, one lone candle appeared. However, this time his 3D viewing accessory made it seem to hover right in front of his face. He tried moving his eyes to left and right, up and down, in an effort to find a corner to obscure his vision. The best result came when he strained his muscles to look straight down. He could still see the candle, but only in his peripheral vision. Perhaps if he stayed like that and kept shouting to cover any sounds, he might get through the ride without losing his mind.

The candle waxed, waned, and was then extinguished. With an audible clunk, a trapdoor opened and Brent's vehicle was lowered down into a sublevel. Darting his eyes round briefly, he saw he was in an empty, dimly lit room. On the far wall was a large viewing window, and through it he could see Marco Scarvetti waving merrily at him. Beside the Sicilian was Carlotta, wearing a white fur coat, and a smaller bald-headed man, his face heavily wrinkled. Standing behind them was Eliza, the security chief.

Scarvetti pressed a button and spoke, his voice coming through speakers. 'Welcome to Track B, Mr Brent. Before I bid you *bon voyage*, I'd like to introduce you to my friend, Jacopo Weidenreich.' He put his arm round the bald man's shoulders. 'He's the engineering genius who made all of this possible.'

'You're insane, all of you!' Brent yelled.

'We're not . . . but you soon might be,' Scarvetti retorted. Eliza leaned forward and said something in his ear. He nodded. 'Unfortunately, time's of the essence, as I believe we've attracted some unwelcome attention at the gates. I'm afraid I can't wait on ceremonies this time, so without further ado . . . ' Grinning fiendishly, he threw a lever forward with a dramatic flourish, and the small car lurched off again into darkness.

Keeping his eyes turned downwards, Brent felt the car move along the track. A great gust of wind blew into his face, stinging his eyes. Then coloured lights started to appear all around him, swirling like a maelstrom. The effect was unnerving, and he felt like he was constantly tipping. The lights then brightened and started to flash rapidly, continuously, spinning all the while. It began to create a strange feeling in his mind, almost as if a door was being forced open against his will. The pressure built until he was sure that something in his brain was going to explode. Then the lights cut out and he was left with only his erratic breathing to break the silence and the after-image of the lights seared into the retinas of his eyes.

Then the sound began.

It started quietly, just a faint drip, drip sound from behind his right ear. It grew insidiously, becoming an ugly, slurping, sloshing, squelching, slobbering, gelatinous noise. There was a smell too — a stomach-churning reek as of something long dead that had been left in a dank cellar to fester.

Brent gulped. His heart was thumping. He felt something wet and sticky touch the back of his neck, and an involuntary shudder ran through him. Then the darkness was banished and all round were images of gigantic, amorphous, slime-covered abominations — unimaginably loathsome things more devastatingly grotesque than the foulest conjurations of mortal madness and morbidity.

Violently, the car went into a corkscrew twist. Screaming, Brent thrashed in his seat, his mind in a pitiful state, balanced on the edge of madness. He became convinced there were things coming for him, reaching out for him. Unearthly things; dead things; wriggling things; burrowing things; cold, damp and tentacled. Dread had become a tangible lump in his chest as he now knew the meaning of real, abysmal fear for the first time in his life. In his mind was a vortex oddly blended of sheer horror and utter revulsion. His heart pumped madly, and there was a roaring in his ears as the blood pounded through his temples. Sweat leaked from his forehead. Fiercely, he tried to raise the safety bar with his thighs, to free himself from this chaos.

Glistening, nightmarishly spawned, slavering terrors poured and seeped down the walls of the tunnel. A bubbling multi-eyed contagion swam into view. The private investigator tried to avoid looking, but the things were everywhere. He kept telling himself that it was only a film, just special effects. Yet the more he saw, the more he became convinced that this was reality; that he had either descended into hell, or else these demons had found some way to break through a dimensional rift into his world. Whether due to the 3D imagery or to the situation itself, it seemed as though these horrors were inside his brain; devouring it, infecting it, draining it.

Stop it! he told himself fiercely. Biting down hard on his bottom lip, enough to draw blood, the pain allowed him to distract himself temporarily from the mind-altering madness, snapping him back into some level of sanity. He drew in a deep breath.

The slime-spewing horrors disappeared. The walls of the tunnel were dark red and pulsed as if blood was pumping through them. The track twisted and turned, canted unnervingly to one side.

Moans and screams, heard at a distance, were accompanied by brief flashes of disjointed, subliminal, Grand Guignol-style phantasmagoria. In contrast to the cosmic horrors of the otherworldly, these new images were morbidly mundane; dreadful visions of death, pain, suffering and perversion that looked all too real to dismiss. There was also a recurring incongruous image of a young attractive blonde woman, not dissimilar to Marilyn Monroe. She appeared and disappeared in snippets obviously taken from a home movie — a wedding scene, happily celebrating a child's birthday party, strolling in a park with a dog, posing on a veranda, smiling from a hotair balloon hundreds of feet above a jungle.

Brent was shaking now. The combination of what he was seeing and hearing had begun to take a serious toll. Whether due to Scarvetti's cunning or just at the suggestion of his beleaguered mind, he started to hear familiar voices. One of them calling for mercy sounded like his sister, and then he thought he heard his mother. A deep stentorian voice suddenly boomed something unintelligible in his ears — a sound unlike anything he had ever heard before. He screamed and started to flick his eyes rapidly to the left and right, trying to blur the images. It was as though his brain were on the verge of shorting out.

Everything went dark. His mouth working madly, Brent started to mumble loudly to himself — reciting bits of poems he remembered from school, reeling off lists of London monuments; anything to take his mind off the hell he was in. Then he found himself upside-down as his vehicle flipped on its track, hanging from the specially designed rails. Dangling like a carcass on a meat-hook, he began to hope that the rush of blood to his head would make him lose consciousness. Then he saw her again, the woman from before. This time she was in a forest, wearing tough hiking gear. She looked around, seemingly unaware of the camera.

The track spiralled round and then proceeded along the level again. Brent hardly noticed. He had guessed that the woman he had seen was Elizabeth Scarvetti — wife of the sick and deranged Sicilian mastermind whose unholy contraption he was now in. She was surrounded by grim-faced men and women who grabbed hold of her and savagely began to tear at her, throwing her to the ground.

The image intensified as the camera zoomed in. Brent knew he was about to witness this woman being eaten alive. And that this was no fakery. This was real. This was the point of no return.

Suddenly, with a deafening bang, the tunnel ceiling collapsed and the right-hand wall disintegrated, creating a huge, gaping hole to the outside world. The car was flung violently from its track as the rail it had been travelling along buckled out of shape; concertinaed into a heap of tangled ruin.

The inner workings of The Horror lay exposed like those of a dissected cadaver. The tunnel floor gave way.

Brent screamed as the vehicle plummeted for a good fifteen feet before striking a portion of lower track, causing more devastation. It then crashed over to one side, the locking mechanism mercifully breaking on impact, throwing its passenger free. He squirmed away, narrowly avoiding a large metal lighting gantry lined with mini-projectors, which smashed down onto the car. The right lens of the peculiar optical device he wore had cracked, causing his vision in that eye to appear frosted, slightly kaleidoscopic.

Flaming detritus — lumps of molten plastic and charred wood — rained from above. A huge fibreglass panel cracked and fell away, revealing more of the attraction's ghastly innards. Several wax dummy props caught fire and began to melt, their hideous faces dribbling horribly in a flow of yellow and scarlet.

From outside, Brent could hear the sounds of voices crying out in Italian, and then there were two smaller explosions and what sounded like sporadic bursts of gunfire. Physically, he was not that badly injured — a cut on his forehead, the only sign that he had by some stroke of luck just escaped a powerful blast. Mentally, however, his mind was still reeling from the sights and sounds of Scarvetti's mind-warping attraction. He was confused and dazed; uncertain as to what had just transpired. Briefly, he found himself entertaining the idea that this latest development was part of the whole experience — wondering if this calamity had its root in reality or whether it was achieved through outstanding special effects.

Someone cried out something, again in Italian. A hand grenade flew into the newly created opening.

'Christ!' Lucidity sped back into Brent's brain. He saw the hurled bomb strike the far wall. It then fell to the floor, disappearing amidst the chaotic jumble of joists, lengths of track, turntables and flaming props. Knowing there was nothing more that he could do, he threw himself flat.

For several heartbeats all was quiet . . . and then the grenade detonated, creating an ear-splitting boom and showering a ten-foot radius with deadly shrapnel, the shockwave itself powerful enough to blast more internal walls asunder.

Scorched and blackened but otherwise uninjured, Brent struggled free of the wreckage. Finding a piece of ruptured track, the edge of which had been sheared off, he quickly managed to cut through his bindings. Tearing the glasses from his face, he dashed them to the floor and trod on them. Rubbing at his eyes, he then clambered his way into the undamaged core of The Horror, any lingering delusions that this was some kind of cinematic experience now gone from his mind. That Screamworld was under direct attack was the only possible explanation, and his only hope of survival lay in getting as far from here as possible. Undoubtedly Zucci and his gangster cohorts where behind this; and if they wanted to reduce the fairground to rubble, and perhaps dispose of Scarvetti in the process, that was their business — one that he was best staying clear of.

A third explosion shook the entire structure. A flask of flaming oil was lobbed inside. It smashed, sending a sheet of liquid fire across the ground. From the melting monsters a dark, acrid smoke began to gather that Brent could almost taste, and the smell was horrendous. Noting the spreading fire, he pushed his way deeper into the heart of the attraction. The going was hard, his movement impeded; for the areas he was entering were dimly lit and the floor was uneven, designed for the small cars, not for walking. Opening a door, he found himself in a stretch of familiar passage, its walls daubed with ghoulish faces all garishly painted with luminous oils. He stopped to listen, fearful of encountering any of Scarvetti's men, well aware that, now that the 'experiment' had been terminated due to outside intervention, he was expendable.

For ten seconds or so, all was quiet. And then the faint report of gunfire started up. It grew louder.

Brent's situation was unbearable. He had to get out of The Horror, but what awaited him upon doing so could prove even worse. If it was Zucci who was behind this campaign of destruction, he had brought with him the muscle and the firepower — automatic weapons, explosives, and Molotov cocktails — to ensure maximum damage. It sounded like World War Three had erupted out there.

Up ahead, Brent saw a door that was slightly ajar. He headed for it, his intuition — that it was a maintenance door — thankfully proving correct; for beyond it lay a normal-looking corridor that terminated in an open door leading to the outside. His guess was that Scarvetti and his cronies had used this route as a means of escape.

More gunfire, further away this time, broke out like distant thunder.

Reaching the exit, Brent looked out nervously. He could see no one. From his admittedly little knowledge of The Horror's layout, he reasoned that he was now at the far side of the ride — to the left of the main entrance and on the opposite side from where he had been accosted by the two 'long-coats' on his first visit. Tongues of fire leapt up the horribly decorated façades, illuminating the surroundings in an infernal glow.

Holding his head, Brent staggered forward. He felt as though he was coming out of a drugged state, his mind still reeling from the sights and sounds he had been subjected to. Unsteadily, he leant against a wall, thought about throwing up, and then managed to take a firmer grip on himself. If he were to get out of this alive, he would have to have all of his wits about him. Over to his right, he heard voices calling. From his concealment, he could see figures moving in the darkness — half a dozen armed men, silhouetted in the glow from the conflagration. They moved forward, heading away from The Horror.

More bullets started to fly. Men screamed. Two were gunned down as the rest ran for cover.

Brent was no hero. And whereas a private investigator from a different era and a different background might well have dashed forward, picked up a fallen gun and joined in the battle, his only concern was getting out and informing the authorities.

Voices called out from nearby.

It would have been suicide for Brent to remain where he was. Stealthily, he edged out from his hiding place, saw that the coast appeared clear, and broke into a sprint for the exit.

The crowds that had been here earlier were replaced with dead bodies. A score or more lay strewn all over. Some were burnt but most had been shot, their corpses bloody. Most of them were 'long-coats', but some were dressed differently. One was Fred Haddow, who had presumably been hanging around Screamworld one last fatal time, and another was Zucci, his body riddled with bullets.

Much of Screamworld was going up in flames. The Death Trap was now a veritable inferno, and as Brent sprinted past, a huge part of the wooden rollercoaster collapsed. And then from some distance beyond it, rising like a phoenix from its ashes, he heard and saw a sleek black twin-seater helicopter take to the air. It banked to one side, allowing him to clearly see its two occupants — Viscero and Eliza — before speeding off. Cursing the fact that those two had escaped, his spirits lifted slightly on seeing the exit just up ahead. It was burning fiercely yet looked passable. He made a run for it.

Suddenly a large part of the outer wall crumbled to the ground. There was a loud burst of machine-gun fire.

Brent stood at the entrance to the theme park. He looked back and, through the pandemonium — the bloodshed and the carnage — he saw Scarvetti. The mad film director was about thirty yards away and had just mown down two of Screamworld's intruders. To make sure his victims were dead, he walked over and murderously sprayed their corpses, emptying a clip of bullets. Casually, he then threw the machine-gun to the ground and drew out a handgun. Noticing the private investigator, he raised his firearm and pulled the trigger.

Brent heard the bang and then the wincing pain as the bullet winged his left thigh. For a moment he was stunned, unable to register the fact that he had been shot. It was only when a second bullet whizzed past his right ear that his survival instincts prompted him to dive for cover behind the parked van that had brought him here. Biting back the pain, he limped, head down, around the side.

'Ruined! Everything's ruined!' Scarvetti called out. 'Those bastards! And where's my back-stabbing son? Abandoned me!' He stood framed in Screamworld's burning gateway like some guardian at the entrance to hell, his face contorted with fury. 'I'll show them all. I'll rebuild it with their corpses. I'll — ' There was a loud crack from directly above him, prompting him to turn and look up.

Brent could not help but watch as the

huge fang-filled sculpture, its mouth agape, fell from the flaming archway. Jaws snapped together like those of some prehistoric carnivore as it smashed down on Scarvetti.

Before Brent looked away, he thought he saw a foot kicking spasmodically amongst the splattered mess.

* * *

George Cavanagh's office was just as it had been when Brent had last stood there a little over a week ago, but both men looked considerably older. They had spoken in hospital, where Brent had spent three nights being checked over, but this was the first time they had really had the chance to talk.

'Have you been given the all-clear?' Cavanagh asked worriedly. He had rushed over to Brent to ease him into a chair when he had limped into the office.

'Physically. Although I keep getting the occasional flashback. The shrink wants to run some tests later, but I may refuse. I'm not sure I want anyone messing with my head again.' Brent's voice was gravelly, a result of the noxious smoke he had briefly inhaled while trapped in The Horror. 'Do you think I could have a cup of coffee?'

'Try this instead.' Cavanagh brought out a bottle of brandy and poured a careful measure. 'It's been a comfort to me these last few days.' He handed Brent a glass.

Brent took a sip, savouring the warming taste. 'Yes, I can see why,' he said wearily. 'Has there been any more news of Mellors?'

'He's still in Queen Charlotte's being treated for respiratory problems, but he should be fine in a couple of weeks. I visited him yesterday, and he's fired up with enthusiasm about his book. Says he has to get it finished quickly before others jump on the bandwagon, now that Screamworld is so infamous.'

The demise of Marco Scarvetti and the destruction of Screamworld had been big news. Adrian Fuller had interviewed Brent in hospital and written a long exposé that had been snapped up by the national newspapers. Despite the late hour of the attack, locals from a nearby village had seen the flames and called the fire brigade. The press had not been far behind, and photographs of the theme park in flames had been on every front page.

'I'm still a bit confused about the Scotland Yard involvement,' Brent said.

'I got the wind up when I hadn't heard from you. The hotel confirmed that you'd left, but when you didn't turn up for our appointment I feared the worst. This time I wasn't going to take no for an answer. I called up my contacts and told them what you'd found out. They agreed to meet with Scarvetti, but it was already too late.'

'Certainly too late for James. It was too late three weeks ago,' Brent agreed sombrely. 'He was in a terrible state. I'm sorry to say it, but I think he made the right choice at the end. It wouldn't have been any kind of life. I hope to God his wife doesn't get to find out about what exactly happened.'

Cavanagh nodded in agreement. 'Still, at least they found Mellors.'

'And he really had no idea about being drugged?'

'None whatsoever. He thought Scarvetti

and that woman had been charming!'

Brent grimaced. 'Well, they were. Up to a point.'

'Do you think Scarvetti was completely mad? That he believed he was anything other than a sadistic torturer?'

It was a question that Brent had gone over more than once since the night he had seen the film director crushed by his own creation. 'On balance, yes. The son was just in it for the money, but Scarvetti was mad enough to believe himself inspired.' He swirled the brandy round in his glass slowly.

'Yes, this Viscero sounds like a nasty piece of work.'

'Have they found him yet?'

'No. MI5 think he's lying low for a while. If he had some kind of deal with the Russians, he may have blown his chances. He can't deliver The Horror; it's just twisted metal and burnt celluloid. He might have enough information about it, and — crucially — back-up copies of the projections to create it again, but we don't know. The agent who debriefed me said that if anything of that kind starts to be hinted at in certain circles, they'll have developed defences against the effects.'

Brent grimaced. 'Good luck to them with that. The only way to survive The Horror, to my mind, is to avoid it in the first place. I was fortunate that this Don Lorenzo character decided to make an example of Scarvetti. Apparently a phone call was put through to Sicily shortly after my meeting with Zucci. Whatever was said then led to Zucci setting out to raze Screamworld to the ground. He just wasn't expecting Viscero to have all his goons there. A few of them survived, and they've been filling in the gaps for the police.' He stopped talking, his throat feeling the strain.

'So what are you going to do now, John?' Cavanagh asked. 'Like I said in the hospital, there's always a job here for you if you want it. It's the least I can do.'

'I might take you up on that sometime, but I'm going to be busy for a while.'

'Of course. You need to recover.'

'True, but I've been offered a short-term job that I really can't turn down.'

'An offer you can't refuse, eh?'

Brent's eyes grew a little less tired, and he almost smiled. 'The government wants to track down Scarvetti's money, which might lead directly to Viscero. As we know that a lot of it was the proceeds of crime they want to claw it back, and I've been offered a healthy percentage. Screamworld burned to the ground, but it seems Scarvetti kept his paperwork in a secret room at his house. One of MI5's men found it when they searched the place, and it looks like Viscero had no idea of its existence. I think we can agree that I'm not cut out to be a man of action, but it'll give me great pleasure to ruin that little bastard in my own way.'

Cavanagh poured another measure of brandy into each of their glasses. 'Well, I can think of no one better to do it.' He raised his glass. 'I wish you every luck with it, for you and for James McAlister.'

Brent raised his glass. 'For James McAlister.' Images of the poor wretch were vivid in his mind and probably would be to the day he died. He remembered his promise to kill Scarvetti — a promise he had been unable to keep; but from his discussions with the secret service, he knew that if they found Viscero he would never see justice in a British court of law. They had kept the details of his claims of selling the torture device to hostile governments out of the papers for fear of causing an international incident. As and when they found him, he would simply be quietly executed, assuming the Mafia did not get to him first.

Revenge on the remaining Scarvetti would come, and Brent would be a part of it. That would have to be enough.

We do hope that you have enjoyed reading this large print book.

Did you know that all of our titles are available for purchase?

We publish a wide range of high quality large print books including:
Romances, Mysteries, Classics
General Fiction
Non Fiction and Westerns

Special interest titles available in large print are:
The Little Oxford Dictionary
Music Book, Song Book
Hymn Book, Service Book

Also available from us courtesy of Oxford University Press:
Young Readers' Dictionary
(large print edition)
Young Readers' Thesaurus
(large print edition)

For further information or a free brochure, please contact us at:
Ulverscroft Large Print Books Ltd.,
The Green, Bradgate Road, Anstey,
Leicester, LE7 7FU, England.
Tel: (00 44) **0116 236 4325**
Fax: (00 44) **0116 234 0205**

SOMETIMES THEY DIE

Tony Gleeson

Detective Frank Vandegraf is familiar with acts of random violence during the committing of a crime; but the street robbery and death of a shady attorney gives him pause, as the victim seems to have been universally despised. As he struggles to make sense of a crime with not enough evidence and too many suspects, he finds he's been assigned a new partner. But before they can acclimatize to each other, the discovery of troubling new information relating to another unsolved assault and robbery will test their ability to work together.

THE MISSING NEWLYWEDS

Steven Fox

Sergeant Sam Holmes and Doctor Jamie Watson have been given what should be a simple case of finding a couple of newlyweds and their limo driver, who disappeared between their wedding reception venue and hotel. Holmes and Watson are puzzled as to why they would be kidnapped without a ransom being asked. On learning that the bride's deceased first husband was an operative for a large private investigative firm who was killed by a drunk driver, they begin to wonder if the case is not part of a wider conspiracy . . .

PRISONER OF KELSEY HOUSE

V. J. Banis

After her ailing, domineering mother dies, Jennifer is invited by relatives she never knew she had to visit them at Kelsey House. But her car stalls on the way there, and the house itself is an eerie old rambling place where it's all too easy to get lost. What's more, every so often a group of ghostly figures dances what might be a child's game, or a primitive rite, on the lawn. What is the secret of Kelsey House and its strange inhabitants — and will Jennifer escape with her life?

MURDER ON LONDON UNDERGROUND

Jared Cade

Peter Hamilton, London Underground's managing director, is horrified when his ex-wife is pushed under a train. Following the murder of a second commuter, he receives an anonymous phone call from an organization calling itself Vortex that is dedicated to preventing the privatization of the network: 'You were the intended victim . . . Next time you won't be so lucky.' Hamilton turns for help to Lyle Revel and Hermione Bradbury, a glamourous couple with a talent for solving murders. But as the death toll rises, the terrorists release a runaway train on the network . . .

STING OF DEATH

Shelley Smith

Devoted wife and mother Linda Campion is found dead in her hall, sprawled on the marble floor, clutching a Catholic medallion of Saint Thérèse. An accidental tumble over the banisters? A suicidal plummet? Or is there an even more sinister explanation? As the police investigation begins to unearth family secrets, it becomes clear that all was not well in the household: Linda's husband Edmund — not long home from the war — has disappeared; and one of their guests has recently killed himself . . .